Serge Joncour was born philosophy at universi become a writer. *UV* i published in Britain. First published September 2003, it won the Prix France Télévisions.

UV

Serge Joncour

*Translated from the French
by Adriana Hunter*

BLACK SWAN

UV
A BLACK SWAN BOOK : 0 552 77249 6

First published in France by Le Dilettante
First publication in Great Britain

PRINTING HISTORY
Black Swan edition published 2005

1 3 5 7 9 10 8 6 4 2

ïï institut français

This book is supported by the French Ministry for Foreign Affairs, as part of
the Burgess programme headed for the French Embassy in London by the
Institut Français du Royaume-Uni.

Set in 11/15pt Melior by
Phoenix Typesetting, Auldgirth, Dumfriesshire.

Black Swan Books are published by Transworld Publishers,
61–63 Uxbridge Road, London W5 5SA,
a division of The Random House Group Ltd,
in Australia by Random House Australia (Pty) Ltd,
20 Alfred Street, Milsons Point, Sydney, NSW 2061, Australia,
in New Zealand by Random House New Zealand Ltd,
18 Poland Road, Glenfield, Auckland 10, New Zealand
and in South Africa by Random House (Pty) Ltd,
Endulini, 5a Jubilee Road, Parktown 2193, South Africa.

Printed and bound in Great Britain by
Cox & Wyman Ltd, Reading, Berkshire.

Papers used by Transworld Publishers are natural, recyclable products made
from wood grown in sustainable forests. The manufacturing processes
conform to the environmental regulations of the country of origin.

UV

Part I

– What will I find in your palace?
– You'll find yourself in my palace and
that will be enough.

Ahmed Séfriouï

It must have been the white that reassured them.

When a stranger pushes open the gates to your property like that, when he is dressed in white from head to foot, and when that white is so absolutely spotless, you don't even think about it being suspicious.

At that time of the afternoon the sun blazed directly on to the terrace, and Julie and Vanessa were the only two who could bear it. Confident that they were alone, they had even slipped off their bikini tops and were sprawled comfortably, thinking only of sunning themselves. In the distance the man paused for a moment, he even had the courtesy to turn his back, revealing the big bag he was carrying over his shoulder, and that too was white. Julie pulled on her blouse, Vanessa wrapped herself in a towel, annoyed to be presenting herself almost naked like this, and actually drawing more attention to her nakedness in her attempts to conceal it.

The man walked towards them with the subtly exaggerated, slightly halting stride of someone who knows they are being watched. His glance flitted from left to right as if he were trying to see every detail of the setting, to take it all in. The images appeared as a series of reflections in the lenses of his Ray-Bans: the emerald green lawn, smooth as velvet; the elegant house built of white stone; the swimming pool at the bottom of a flight of steps; the transparent inflatable chairs undulating on its surface; the teak sun loungers, also unoccupied; evidence of a supremely casual acceptance of luxury bordering on negligence – an atmosphere in which he felt completely at home.

Had they ever seen him before? They both tried to think, but came up with nothing, and had little more idea of what might have inspired him to come here. It must be the beach, no, perhaps the boat.

What tipped them in favour of treating him politely was the consideration he showed in pushing up his sunglasses; it was thoughtful, or at least it showed that he didn't want to distress them any further by concealing his eyes. Especially as those eyes were undoubtedly the second irresistible element of his appeal: acid blue and very direct, the sort of eyes you tear yourself away from with an obscure sense of guilt for avoiding them.

The man made his way towards Vanessa quite naturally, as if they already knew each other, showing no sign of embarrassment or effrontery, facing directly into the glare of the sun.

Now he had to lose himself once again in the complicated strategy of false modesty, to rein in the stealthy hostility that sometimes starts simmering immediately. He had to feign those vital backward steps that might magnify the other person's intentions, to break away from the situation before returning to it. And all the time he was gripped by his ability to please: he had to find the right balance between tact and determination . . .

Philip was not there, so the girls tried to guess when he might arrive. Tomorrow, this evening, later on this afternoon perhaps; you never know with him, anyway . . . Their words betrayed their brother's patchy reliability, without actually complaining about it, without being overly critical.

But he did tell me . . .

Well, yes, that's just like him . . .

There was a plaintive note of courtesy in their replies, the implication that they regretted having to disappoint him, perfectly aware that he had come so far. The man introduced himself: Boris. The name meant something to them, then when he mentioned the school, the years compromised by the near imprisonment, all the clichés about boarding-school life, they recognized some of the chilling memories they had heard from their brother, those painful years spent rebelling against discipline, a whole structure of propriety and civilities that nevertheless produced absolutely no result . . . his absence right now seemed to prove that.

A brief peal of laughter rippled round, giving them a chance to relax. There is always a slight tension when people meet for the first time, especially in circumstances like these. He could already tell that his gambit had worked perfectly. A brief introduction, a couple of anecdotes, making sure he didn't look at the rest of them but only directly into their eyes, he was sailing through the preliminaries.

Of the two sisters it was Julie who seemed to be the most understanding, or at least the most concerned by the situation.

'Let's see, his flight left Newport on the tenth, and I know he wanted to spend a couple of days in New York . . .'

'Either way, he'll be here for the fourteenth of July,' Vanessa said a little sharply, irritated by her

13

sister's unnecessary openness and affability.

She immediately regretted saying that, annoyed with herself because she could see she had succeeded in giving them the perfect transition in their conversation. And there was Julie waxing lyrical with every kind of detail about the fourteenth of July, explaining that every year Philip insisted on setting off his fireworks on the southernmost tip of the island, thereby gratifying all the holidaymakers in the area as well as the family; and he was particularly unlikely to want to miss this ceremony – idolatrous and widely accepted though it was – because it gave him a unique opportunity to shine, to show there was at least something he could do really well. The fourteenth of July was his moment of glory . . .

Boris tried to imagine the ambiguous pleasure that might be derived from toying with all this, the multicoloured explosives, the detonations amplified by the echo from the cliffs, the showering reflections over the whole bay, the squeals and general delight that it would surely create . . .

Still sitting, Vanessa clutched her towel to herself as if she were cold, moving as little as possible, afraid to expose herself in any way. She was, in fact, completely consumed by the thought of the dressing down she would give her brother: even though she'd been turning a blind eye to his fecklessness for some time, this time he had overstepped the mark. Dumping a stranger on them like this, without any warning, and they didn't even know how to get hold of him, having been left with a number that didn't ring, clearly implying he hadn't paid the bill. Yet again this was verging on the irresponsible . . . And here she was again, resenting him, daydreaming about putting him in his place. As her anger overrode her anxiety, she started looking forward to the tongue-lashing she would give him as soon as he arrived.

With people close to you, you start worrying quite quickly if they don't answer their mobile – that pointless ringing in a vacuum, all the inevitable fears awakened by the situation, thinking the worst; but with Philip this was practically normal, just another sign of his fecklessness, of the permanent adolescence he wallowed in.

Behind her superficial smile, Vanessa could now think of only one thing: having him at her mercy and telling him a few home truths. They were all a little too ready to think of Philip's flippancy as part of his character (if not, actually, a good quality), and even if all the others had resigned themselves to her brother's unreliability, she herself had not lost all hope of changing him.

'You wouldn't happen to have something to drink?'

'Of course. Vanessa, would you . . . ?'

Vanessa threw a venomous glance at her sister,

infuriated by her imperious tone, proof that this stranger's mere presence was enough to make her lose her composure and grasp for control of the situation. She clamped her towel to her and stood up without a word, overwhelmed by the feeling of a ruined afternoon, by the infuriating circumstances that sometimes conspired – like a spell cast over her – so that she knew she would never get a moment's peace.

As he realized how thirsty he actually was, he thought back over his whole journey, as if that thirst had been the one constant throughout. The hurried departure, the heady feeling of setting off, all those different times along the way he had asked for a glass of water, the aftertaste of chlorine as he put it back down – always the same whatever tap it had come from, the one in the motorway service station or the one in the toilets at the port, carafes of water in cafés or the spurt of a water fountain – and his difficulty at each stage as he tried to find his way, reconstituting the route from what the other man had told him.

Julie revelled in the feeling of having this man standing over her, she played on her advantage of being on her own territory, not so much arrogant or contemptuous, just enjoying the private pleasure of dominating someone, manipulating them into asking permission for the least thing. As a child this characteristic had made her obnoxious: she would use the weekends as opportunities to invite schoolfriends home, just for the perverse pleasure of ruling over them all. It was then that, without asking permission of any sort, Boris pulled up a chair and sat down. He lowered his glasses for a moment and Julie caught sight of herself in the reflection, a fleeting image that disturbed her, sending a shiver down her spine, a glimpse of herself looking dazed. She quickly sat up.

His self-assurance, the way he hadn't even asked, the way he refused to play along with her little game, appealed to her, she liked the fact that a man could display that sort of impertinence. She could already imagine the subtle pleasure, the triumph, of unsettling this man, of finding some way to make him feel uncomfortable.

Vanessa reappeared on the steps having clearly redone her hair, and with a pareo secured around her chest. She held the glass out to Boris with no niceties beyond a tight smile. It was a simple glass of grenadine, which he took carefully as if it were a trophy. These few millilitres he held in his hand, this precious liquid, was a measure of the time he had left to convince them. So long as this glass was not empty he would still have a pretext to stay, bearing in mind that the last ferry left the island at eight o'clock. Before even bringing it to his lips he rolled the glass in his hand for a long time, cooling himself with it, even bringing it up to his cheek, then he held it out in front of him, the red so absolutely liquid and so absolutely red, like everything he could see through it: the house, the grounds, all of it undulating in a nebulous red, the swimming pool, the sea beyond, the whole scene drowned in pomegranate, in the juice of this crushed fruit he had been offered . . . unable to hold out any longer, he downed the glass in one and re-emerged from it with a sigh. With the speed of an involuntary reflex, he asked if he could have another.

Vanessa was surprised at this urgency, a boorishness only just defused by his cheerful smile.

To Julie he was just thirsty.

'Well, aren't you going to get him another one?'

Every time the heat descended like this, as suffocating as a noxious gas, the ironmonger worried
about having all this stuff on his premises. What he
found really daunting were the red stencilled
letters, the word *danger* stamped all over the
things. The compensation for his anxiety, the
reward for this ordeal, was that the commission
would be good. Every year he sold them on – these
rockets of his – with a more than comfortable
margin, an unusually high margin even, for a
simple ironmonger. And the fireworks were over-
priced in the first place . . .

The other compensation was the front-row seats,
because the Chassagnes always invited him and
his wife to watch the display, it was one way they
could join the ranks of the lucky few, seeing the
fireworks from the best vantage point. Still, until
Philip – the Pyro, as they called him in private –
came and took this arsenal off his hands, he knew
he would not sleep well.

*   *   *

There would be a firework display in town, too, but that one would be a communal affair, feeble rockets set off several minutes apart by cheery firemen, and the exaggerated 'oohs' of a sarcastic audience, a caricature of splendour. Compared to that, the display put on by the Chassagne boy seemed somehow provocative, a sort of aristocrat's fourteenth of July. The supreme grandeur of this ballet of sparks, the waves of twinkles over the mirror of the sea, the fountains of strident colour over the pink granite of the cliffs, was a very different story from the solid reds and blues down in the port . . . Two or three half-cut firemen, glibly confusing cans of beer with tubes of fireworks, taking the cap off one and sipping the other, so that the rockets sometimes fell somewhat flat, producing beerworks rather than fireworks, beautiful reds, which flared up limply with a wheezy green burping over the top of them, and so on until everyone felt dispirited or fed up, just waiting for that last one that was constantly postponed though everyone almost longed for it.

That is why when night fell on the fourteenth of July quite a few people from Paimpol would keep one eye on the north, some of them even going so far as to hop into a boat for a closer view. I mean, given how costly fireworks are, you

20

might as well go and watch a rich man's display.

Another few days of knowing he had all this under his roof, enough to blow the place up, the whole street even, a real textbook case for the firemen.

When he heard the first notes of a piece of music coming from the sitting room and saw the two sisters waving to someone behind him, Boris stood up, expecting to be introduced to someone.

Once again he would have to put on a good show; combine the correct elements of that first impression; apply himself to the subtle window-dressing that can make someone find you instantly agreeable, welcome anywhere; to find the right words once more; to affect that little air of awkwardness – not too much, though, so as not to appear embarrassed; to distil enough pertinence and humour from the conversation to ease the atmosphere . . . a prodigious effort when all was said and done. Over time, he had mastered that skilful formula somewhere between shyness and confidence, humility and self-satisfaction.

There was nothing solemn about the father's greeting – in fact it was warm. It was the greeting of a man of advanced years who has grown serene with the passing of time, a patriarch who has acquired the vice of seeing everything in the best possible light, and who sees every little surprise, every unexpected visit, as another excuse to give thanks to fate. Especially as this stranger standing in front of him, this man with the firm handshake and the steady gaze, was someone of whom he had already decided he would approve.

The soprano soared through the octaves on the quadraphonic sound system in the sitting room. The father was a music lover, and he modulated one hand, stilling it through the silences as if expecting some sort of approval or comment on the performance. Even if Boris did recognize the aria, he would not have been able to say which opera it was from – a shortcoming that would not be to his credit and that persuaded him to avoid the subject.

But the father did want to speak about it. For him this piece of music was something of a ritual, one that marked the end of his siesta, a reminder of the sun still shining behind the shutters, a renewed enthusiasm for a summer not yet over that was still very much there, the scent of the sea captured in full flow, and of the wind driving it on, and that predictable reflex to scan the whole expanse of the sky yet again, all this came back to him as a sympathetic response . . . the father emerged from his siesta as if coming back to life. Boris, who had given up his chair to the older man, was now looking directly at the house and could quite openly examine it at his leisure. Without turning around, the father launched into a description of the house, his voice glowing with the undying enthusiasm of one still captivated by it. According to him it was an example of petit-Trianon style, like the smaller of the two palaces at Versailles. It was built in white freestone, a kind of limestone, which had had to be brought a long way to get there, apparently on the whim of one of his fore-fathers, who – by choosing not to conform by using the customary local pink granite – had hoped to show a degree of originality, a spirit of resistance.

From where he was standing, Boris could see the entrance hall, beautiful pieces of furniture bask-ing comfortably in the liquid light, the perfect disposition of various ornaments, the ultimate refinement achieved by this conjugation of just one style. Through the french windows at the far end of the hall he could see the parkland extending, uninterrupted, on the far side of the house. The music was coming from a little sitting room on the left.

'The limpid harmonies and those soft soprano notes . . . there's nothing quite like it for bringing you round from a siesta. Most sopranos wear their voices out on that passage. But then, that's what's difficult about this piece: starting with the high point, the apotheosis. And you, were you in the choir at Buzenval?'

Boris replied with a little laugh that was intended to be affirmative.

'And you didn't suffer too much there? I mean at boarding-school, of course, the discipline, the regulations . . . ?'

How could anyone not suffer? Boarding-school is always experienced as a constraint, an exclusion or – why not say it? – an imprisonment. The morning services; the evening prayers; the mediocre food; the sense that your freedom is constantly held in check by the fences round the grounds; the long, freezing dormitories, communal rooms where there was no privacy except inside the mind (that was the worst of it); a very dilute kind of prison . . .

'And it must have been difficult not seeing your parents . . .'

'Yes. That too.'

Boris was annoyed he had not thought of that himself.

'As far as Philip is concerned, I'm very afraid that it was a mistake to leave him stewing there for all those years, nearly eight years. We thought the discipline would build up his character, that some time boarding would balance out his complacency, but – instead – the whole episode just made him acrimonious, more rebellious. I'm very afraid that it made him lose any sense of judgement, perhaps

25

even his mind . . . Well, at least while he was there he had the chance to meet you. Every cloud has a silver lining, as they say.'

In these words Boris recognized that elegance, that ultimate refinement of knowing how to conclude a subject by flattering your listener, an implacable form of courtesy that he would have to match.

'And you, Boris, have you ever been to the United States?'

Again that moment's calculation to set up his reply correctly, but the father was interrupting him already.

'But, what a bore the place is, with its endless roads, the people all talking too quickly, hassling you about every little thing, and they don't even have decent terraces in front of the cafés for a bit of a rest, frankly it's a nightmare . . . As for the countryside, well, what can I say? Obviously they have that too, but – like everything else – on such a huge scale that you get bored of it, the only parts of the United States that I like are the ones that remind me of France—'

This made the two girls burst out laughing, that sort of irrepressible laughter, which – if you are not sharing in it – can very quickly make you feel as if it is at your expense. The father patted Boris's leg, admitting that this was his favourite trick, his weakness perhaps: fabricating . . . In fact, he had never set foot in the United States, not out of some systematic aversion, but because he was afraid of flying. All he knew of the country was what he had seen in films. And it was a family game, a form of entertainment, inventing anecdotes, making up stories about everything and anything, it was rather fun, especially at the moment, given that it's the holidays, don't you think?

This sort of gentle mystification counted amongst their hobbies, and they went about it with the same careful application as if they had been creating something as delicate and potentially dangerous as a firework. Just like the fact that Philip was not there. After all, that too could have been a joke, perhaps he had actually been there all along, he was hiding somewhere in one of the upstairs rooms with the shutters closed, or in the sitting room downstairs, turning up the volume . . . He probably thought it was a good idea to let his little prank run on for a while, so that he could really catch out his old room-mate, his fellow sufferer in detention, letting him marinade in this tolerable situation for a good half-hour, just to see . . .

With this, Boris started to feel slightly uneasy, even though he realized that this climate of game-playing at his expense, this strong hand played him by the father, had defused Vanessa's suspicious attitude towards him. Having laughed at him so wholeheartedly had in some ways made her feel closer to him.

'You went to law school yourself, didn't you?'

Without waiting for a reply, the father was already giving his commentary, pointing out that, as far as being a lawyer was concerned, Philip was now nothing more than an extremely accomplished student, and that he must be in about his tenth year of studies, or placements, or whatever it was.

'Well, at least he'll be absolutely bilingual by the end of it, which – given his abilities – is in itself quite an achievement.'

Now he was no longer joking, he seemed to be experiencing a surge of the existential disillusion that a son can inflict when he fails, a feeling of unfairness mingled with regret for the mistakes he the parent may have made; but also a tinge of indulgence because – however prodigal and undeserving a son may be – the parents always try to find a way to remove some of the blame from him, even if it means shouldering a share of the responsibility themselves. The indulgence here was all the more obvious as the son in question was not even there to hear it.

'It's such a shame for the Estate, you see. Being bilingual isn't enough when it comes to running more than a hundred hectares of vineyards . . . or even being a lawyer, you'll probably tell me. But anyway, tell me, what is it that you do?'

Boris replied solemnly that he lived by his wits and off stolen goods, he didn't do badly on thin air either, perhaps the odd scam if he could dig one up, but the bulk of his work was still the narcotics trafficking . . . Amongst his increasingly perplexed audience, the father was the first to respond with laughter, nodding appreciatively at his guest's wit, and concluding that they should get along very well indeed.

One-nil.

Boris mentally chalked up his score.

The two sisters had gone in to change.

They only reappeared when the shouts rang out from the swimming pool. From the doorway they could see the father frantically smacking the water as if trying to get some purchase on the surface, while his feet were wedged in the armrests of the inflatable chair. Boris was powering through the water beneath him like a shark, a shadow distorted by the ripples . . . Vanessa ran over, screaming that her father was drowning, and it was just as she was preparing to dive in that Boris reappeared with the father on his shoulder, the old man gasping in air like a tuna fish hoisted out of the water, so short of breath that he was almost blue in the face, the old man who was already laughing and swearing that everything was fine, that it was nothing, nothing but a joke that he'd played on himself, an unwise one perhaps given that he had sworn he would never get on to those ridiculous chairs again, that he was too old for it, but, well, young Boris here was so enthusiastic he'd persuaded him to have a swim . . .

Having felt this man quivering between his hands, having carried him in his arms, Boris was reminded of the nights he had spent calming the other, not – in all honesty – out of humanity but rather for some peace, so that he could get some sleep, especially as at the beginning Philip had cried the whole time. At first he had been tough with him, almost brutal, but he had very quickly changed his approach, more out of pity than compassion. That's the way it is, the beefcakes always feel a need to adopt the more vulnerable, creating a stranglehold in which the protégé gains in protection what the other establishes in power, a sort of ascendancy bordering on filiation in the best cases, and domination in the worst.

Once they had recovered from the commotion, Boris and the father drank to each other's health, clashing their glasses together forcefully, and they had hardly swallowed their second Martini and orange before the father was suggesting they tried Martini and tonic with a dash of lemon and a bit of gin next time. As part of the game, Boris watched the father and felt he could read him quite clearly. The pompous public smile, the supremely steadfast attitude, he was the sort of man who was about as far from being conventional as he was perfectly distinguished, observing the world with a disillusion that bordered on amusement, a detachment derived from the relativity all things acquire once they are viewed from the great height of advanced years. His dignified bearing revealed the attributes of true distinction, the pointed chin, the stiff neck carriage, and the gaze, so direct, unhindered, the expression of those who have spent their lives looking far into the distance over their extensive estates or their own convictions, as far as the furthest reaches of their ancestry or their surroundings, people who can take in great expanses of scenery with one look knowing that it is all theirs – how gratifying the countryside becomes once it is surrounded by your own fences! He was one of those people for whom the horizon becomes confused with their own land, the *comfortably off* as they say, and they are loathsome for it, for the strength they derive from knowing the world is theirs, give or take a few hectares, that arrogance too of not even condescending to be accurate . . .

The simple fact of being there, the simple fact of landing quite comfortably in these surroundings, meant claiming them as his own to some extent. A simple effort of imagination and this swimming pool was his. Taking a dip in it whenever the fancy took him was in itself a gauge of progress, a perfectly natural appropriation, when just an hour ago it would have smacked of trespassing.

It is in these circumstances that the expression, the formula trotted out on so many occasions, 'make yourself at home' proves to be an instruction that should never be taken literally. The father had already said – on the subject of the drinks, when he invited him to pour himself another – do please make yourself at home.

Now that he had had a good look at it, he realized he had not pictured the villa like this. Usually you imagine things to be better than they actually are, partly because they are always described in the most positive light but also because the imagination does its fair share of additional work. But for once the opposite was true. He had seen it in his mind's eye a thousand times, but not as big. Just as he had not suspected that there would be the steps leading down from the front door and carrying on into the depths of the pool, nor had he pictured the mosaic blurred by the water, a series of fading blues undulating in an unpredictable pattern, the surface levelled so that it appeared to overflow and lead the eye beyond its borders, so that once you were in the water the pool seemed to merge into

33

the horizon, and the sea was just an extension of its rippling waters.

For more than 180° the edge of the lawn was defined by the cliffs, beyond which the panorama extended over the whole bay. Gliding over the calm waters, the last ferry of the day was making for the island. Its return trip would be the last journey to the mainland. Shielding his eyes with his hand, the father tried to see whether Philip was aboard, believing he recognized him in the tall figure standing on the foredeck. Boris made no move, he didn't even look up.

Oh no.

It's not him.

Pity.

The question of dinner never even arose. Or at least it was quickly answered. The mother experienced the presence of this friend of Philip's as a forerunner to her son's arrival, and she already fluttered with a powerful sense of anticipation. This boy represented the return of her prodigal son, he proved how imminently they would be reunited, especially as she was planning to use the opportunity to get him to talk a little, to clarify the fragments of mystery that hovered around him, the absences and difficult phases that punctuated his life.

Boris felt almost embarrassed that she had been won over so quickly, she had kissed him on both cheeks straight away, and had held on to his arm for some time as she talked to him. He was not used to being outrun on the path that one person treads towards another. To him this family configuration was the ultimate exoticism: this arrangement in which people are at their most docile, their most vulnerable too, ripe for the picking.

*　　*　　*

Two parasols in cream canvas had been put up
over the terrace. The table was laid and covered in
a big white table-cloth, but – even though everything was impeccable – this was not the best dinner
service, the father even apologized for the fact,
guilty of failing in the honours due to any distinguished guest. Boris patted him amicably on the
back, and knocked back the aperitif he had just
topped up.

It was such a warm evening, their clothes were
nothing more than a gauzy layer floating over warm
skin. They each had the idea of pulling up the
edge of some piece of clothing to fan themselves,
catching the least breath of air. André-Pierre did
not feel like that. André-Pierre was there to eat.
André-Pierre had his shirt collar buttoned up
because there was a button there for that very
purpose.

Earlier he had shaken this stranger's hand with
the same aloofness, the same disapproval, he
would demonstrate towards his brother-in-law
when he appeared, particularly as this Boris was
not only a friend of Philip's but he also displayed
the insolence, the casual arrogance, that exudes
from any white shirt once it is left open to reveal a
bronzed torso, one of those torsos with an
unseemly relief of muscled ridges and curves, not
ashamed to be displayed in public. To many

people, this would be a minor detail. André-Pierre, on the other hand, could see nothing else, nothing but this proffered chest and the indecent way it was exhibited, as if displaying a body was something to be proud of. He himself disliked the seaside for this very reason, as indeed he disliked the sun; in fact, he never went down to the beach, never swam, if only to avoid being confronted with this sort of bronzed shamelessness . . . And here he was with one of these specimens thrust under his nose, with one of these casually posing bathers plonked down at the same table as him. On top of that he had even been seated opposite this intruder who was all the more irritating because this evening he was enjoying all the prestige of being a novelty: the others were paying him an excessive amount of attention, laughing at his least utterance, attending to his least wish, he was amusing them all already.

The fact that Vanessa had taken an absurdly long time getting ready this evening had not escaped him. She had even put on make-up as if they were going out. As for Julie, don't let's talk about her. On top of her mania for short skirts, she had adopted a way of walking, a dubious languor, which not only hid nothing of her legs but also gave plenty of scope for imagining the bits that could not be seen. André-Pierre (who knew the two sisters well, and also knew the suspect sense of humour that sometimes gripped his wife's family, their perilous taste for practical jokes) went so far as to persuade himself that they had challenged each other to see which of them would be the more seductive this evening – the sort of game to which their characters disposed them very well.

All the little things André-Pierre no longer bothered with came back to him, his negligence towards his wife as well as his sister-in-law, not even trying to amuse them any more or divert them from some unlikely moment of boredom (particularly as he felt it was highly improbable that a mother of three-year-old twins should have any opportunity to be bored). In the two weeks they had been there, he had never deigned to take the boat out, and – as the father was too old to handle it now – the yacht had stayed in the harbour, not even at anchor but properly moored up. As for the Riva, it never came out of the boathouse, definitively writing off any possibility of a spin out at sea or water-skiing. Which meant that this sea that was right there under their noses, this sea that – only a few years ago – suggested itself as a permanent playground, a space to be conquered and carved through in every direction, had now been reduced to a medium for their absent-minded contemplation, a source of pleasure to be drawn from gazing at it while sitting safely at the water's edge, remembering past outings . . . The only form of entertainment left to them was the swimming pool. Of course there was the beach below, just down from them, but – added to the inconvenience of being amongst the crowds – there was the sense of doing what everyone else was doing. Climbing over those bodies in order to get to the waves, sacrificing modesty in a communion of blubbery flesh, absent-mindedly leafing through a novel in that atmosphere of passing time. That was why the girls no longer went there, unless it was in the cool of the evening, once the bodies had been cleared up and the parasols packed away. As children, they had spent all their holidays on that beach. Whole summers spent swimming in the seaweed and sifting sand, and, because in the early days there had been neither the swimming pool nor the boat, because – at the time – money was used only for sensible things, the beach really had been the only form of entertainment.

Halfway through the meal Boris thought he might casually roll a joint at the table. The girls would probably not be averse to having a smoke; the stuffed shirt, on the other hand, would choke on it. The parents would definitely be perplexed. He tapped the little pouch discreetly on Julie's thigh. She glared at him, almost panicking: later perhaps, when the three of them were together.

From time to time Boris gazed at Vanessa, fascinated by the balanced tableau: she sat with a child on either side of her, running her hands through their hair with the sort of rounded, silky movement he would have liked to experience himself. André-Pierre had noticed this, he was watching for the slightest complicity between them, the slightest glance, seeing whether they already knew each other and were making an effort not to give anything away . . . Another of his idiotic worries, he just had this way of getting in a stew about everything, but half a Temazepam and it'll pass . . . He had his children there to reassure him, her children just as much as they were his, even if he sometimes couldn't quite believe it.

He did not like this man, it was something of a foregone conclusion. He even felt a certain nostalgia for the previous day's meals, those cherished times when it had been just them, when any obligation to say anything had been replaced by the easy silence of familiarity. Only yesterday the dinner table had been perfectly harmonious, lulled by the clinking of plates, compliments on the food, a few vague nothings about the children, while this evening the table was peculiarly animated, boisterous as a banquet. The presence of one new guest had been enough to infect the peaceful atmosphere that had reigned before, especially as it was hotter than ever, as if everything were conspiring to keep everyone outside, lingering at the table. The father had picked up the thread of his stories, the girls were adding their own anecdotes (each more conclusive than the last), the mother would not stop smiling, even the children seemed to be contaminated by the spectacle of people talking to each other. Unless it was due to the application with which Boris kept pouring more wine for everyone, grasping the bottle as if it were his own, urging them to drain their glasses before filling them again, with no hint of class and precious little courtesy, but an edge of authority.

What André-Pierre found most intolerable was the presumptuous way he addressed everyone, and spontaneously called the parents-in-law 'Mum' and 'Dad', whereas he, after more than eight years of marriage to their daughter, still could not manage it. There was also his constant smile, irksome as a flashing light. Especially as he never stopped using his teeth, even if it was just to smile at Vanessa, about anything and everything. She might have just been holding out her glass to him, and he would smile at her. Sometimes he even made her laugh out loud; just by saying thank you he could make her laugh.

This atmosphere of automatic courtesy, of excessive friendliness, eventually unsettled him as much as a bout of indigestion. He even resented his children for laughing at the idiotic faces the man pulled, oh yes, this Boris talked to them too, enough to make you think he was hoping to work his charm on them as well, to conquer them to some extent. In fact, they were so enthusiastic there was no holding them back now. Their giggles swooped over the gathering with an added note of hysteria, an extra curtain of sound overlaying the entire conversation. At one point Boris slipped his hand under a table napkin, creating a makeshift puppet, which produced shrieks of delight and fear from them, absolutely unbearable shrieks . . . And even though they were quite clearly kicking up an infernal racket, even though they kept knocking over glasses and had not touched their pudding, no one was taking them in hand, not the slightest reprimand. It was André-Pierre who sliced through the fun with a barked 'that's enough', his voice so harsh that Boris took it to mean him too, not really surprised that the other man had finally flown off the handle.

The two little faces stayed frozen in an expression of terror, an incredulous 'Oh', ready to dissolve, as the children sounded out the adults' faces to see whether they should laugh or cry.

The father, the mother, the sisters, everyone had some brief reproachful word, saying they hadn't been doing any harm, it was the holidays after all. The grandfather even pushed the conceit so far as to attempt the trick with the puppet himself with his own napkin . . . Seeing this, André-Pierre stood up and left the table, piecing together an implacable expression on his face.

'Come on now, AP, don't go,' Boris said, as if talking to a timid child.

It almost made him lose his footing.

He was calling him AP now.

At this time in the evening the sea undulates gently in the felty darkness, the waves break listlessly on the shore, some of them fizzling up as far as the pebbles, smoothing the sand further up the beach, rinsing the coast of the oils and creams deposited on it throughout the day, purging the memory of those bodies oozing with suncream and sweat. One night to recover, endlessly repeating the polishing, and restoring the glittering dew of dawn; Eden once more.

Once the last ferry had left, the island bestowed its peace on the few islanders. There were not many who really lived there, a chosen few who slept there, especially as there was only one hotel, and the camp site had closed.

On top of the nocturnal exodus, the islanders were duty bound to obscure all light, particularly on the seaward side, and to avoid using any lights out of doors. When night fell here there was not a single street light along the roads, not so much as a lightbulb outside, the houses were lit as little as possible, the shutters were tightly shut. All these measures were taken to avoid disrupting navigation, confusing the trajectories of boats trying to negotiate the channel round the island, between the shallows and the reefs. Beyond this indecipherable sea, lost in shadows, the land itself was dark and impenetrable, every footfall quavering at the possibility of getting lost or falling in the dark. Here the darkness fell as sheer as a cliff, only the moon occasionally picking out contours, but that night there was no moon.

'Why don't we go for a little walk?'

What surprised them in the first instance was that anyone could think that the villa didn't have everything anyone needed to amuse oneself for an evening. In the glow of candlelight the two sisters caught each other's eye questioningly, before consulting the father who was also hesitating. Eventually, as they were not really ready to go to bed yet, they all shifted from perplexed indecision to enthusiasm, each picking up this little phrase and batting it back to the others with increasing conviction: well, why not, after all.

'Unless you're afraid of the dark . . .'

He was the one putting them on their guard. He was the one speaking as if he were familiar with the island, could gauge its every danger and knew its layout.

45

Right, good, just time to put a few things away. At one point, he thought about their swimming things, in case the water was not too cold, but in the end he did not mention them, it would be more fun to improvise.

From his room André-Pierre could clearly make out the preparations, he felt a certain cowardliness for not joining them, not going for the walk, but to be honest the Temazepam dulled the sensation, he was happy in his room, with a good book and cool sheets. As they walked away into the distance, the sound of the sea mingled with their voices, then the voices disappeared, only the sea was left.

'Sometimes, when I'm walking like this, the refrain comes back to me as clearly as if I were really listening to it . . . *Chaste goddess who touches the leaves with silver, turn your cloudless face unto us* . . . What's the next bit?'

Boris had no idea. He was only half listening to the father's monologue, more absorbed by the two white smudges moving in front of them, in front of him. As soon as they were a little way ahead, the two figures merged into one, a white shape swaying magically in the darkness. From time to time they would stop to let the men catch up, pointing out the faint glow from a cargo ship, a lighthouse in the distance, a shooting star, then, when they were still a good distance away, they would set off again.

Only too happy to be reviving the habit of walking after a meal, the father would not stop talking, never doubting that his guest was listening attentively, taking his arm every now and then, lurching on the rugged surface of the steep path and gazing up at the stars.

'. . . The fact that the chaste goddess isn't with us this evening, that she won't grant us so much as a blink, is a bit disturbing, don't you think?'

Boris nodded doubtfully, fascinated by the sea below, churning but invisible.

'The insolence of these astral bodies. I must say, just because they know they'll outlive us . . . But, to get back to *Norma*, apparently the school used to put on a production every year for the charity fête . . .'

'Yes. Every year.'

'What a pity I never saw it. But, well, at the time all I did was send a cheque each term and, given how much it cost, I felt I was offering him the best education available. I'm sure your parents would have been under the same illusion . . . By the way, you are descended from people who were exiled in 1917, aren't you?'

Boris was always brought up short by personal questions, he took a ridiculously long time to answer them, completely unused to confiding in anyone, unless it was to create a diversion, dot a few clues about, establish some premise. The two girls had gone on well ahead of them. After dinner Boris had noticed how avidly they drew on the joint, smiling voraciously but at the same time looking worried, finding it too strong but still inhaling willingly. Since then he had been quietly watching them, keeping an eye on them as they evolved. They were holding each other by the waist, exchanging conspiratorial whispers and occasionally bursting out laughing. They had probably talked about him, but no one should ever be afraid of the impression they give, they should instigate it. It could well be that they were already grateful to him, after all it was thanks to him that this walk had been made possible again, that the night was serving some other purpose than just recovering from the day. It was a long time since they had done this little trip round the island because of the enveloping darkness, the changing tides that redesigned the shoreline, an obscure algebra of coefficients covering the stretches where you were in your depth, an equation of dangers that the father had always harped on about in his excessively alarmist way to try and discourage them from going off alone, especially as he no longer considered himself a sufficiently stalwart rampart to protect them. When it came to going for walks on their own, they would never take the risk, even if just to avoid worrying the others.

'Well then, why on earth did they give you a Russian name?'

'That's another story . . .'

'I see . . . It seems odd that they put you in a

Catholic institution. But, tell me, as we're talking about school, apparently Philip played the title role one year, at least that's what he told me. It is true, isn't it?'

'Of course it's true.'

'But why him in that role?'

'Because there weren't any girls. But he was perfect in it, believe me . . . I'm sure you can see him in the long, peaceful passage, with all of us cooing the refrain, just like earlier, the notes were like liquid, magnificent, you can't imagine . . . And he had such a high voice at the time, and a way of moving about the stage, like a miniature grown-up, you believed it was real. I swear to you that he was the star that day, in fact we even thought he'd make a career of it . . .'

The girls were so far ahead they could no longer see them. The father, still deeply affected, rendered speechless for a while, held Boris's arm all the more firmly, as if expressing his gratitude, as if he had just experienced a rare moment of satisfaction with regard to his son, the first for a long time. For once someone had spoken of him in a positive light, and – what was more – with that surreptitious affection, that unspoken respect, which exists between two long-term friends, two men now. Sensing this, sensing that the father was so moved by the image of his son on the stage, Boris went on in the same vein.

'. . . And you know the bit when it all goes quiet, the passage when the violins surge and fade, more and more slowly, a bit like the sea you could say, yes, something like that, like the sea, a really calm sea, which then stops . . . Well, that was when he started again, he held his note for as long as possible, as if his pride depended on it, as if to dominate us all . . . We really liked him, you know; I promise you, we all really liked him . . .'

The father was disturbed to hear a slight tremor in this strapping young man's voice, a faltering tinged with premonition . . .

Julie's white dress reappeared in the distance, at the very edge of the landmass. Out to sea the signals from boats traced a perfect constellation, like the one above, as limpid and uneven, as if on that night the stars were nothing more than boats, navigating just as happily in the waters below as they did overhead.

As they reached the girls, the father commented on how radiant they seemed this evening, it was a long time since he had seen them sparkling and happy like this. However hard he tried to talk about other things, to appear as detached as possible, he was still dogged by remorse, haunted by the ghost of these memories he did not have of his son, the remorse of never having seen him in such a favourable light, of never having had an opportunity to be proud of him. Philip in a production of *Norma*, that was the most glorious image he had of him to date, and it had taken a complete stranger to reveal it to him.

They were now at the northernmost point of the island, that last finger of land pointing out to sea. The rocks below were hard to distinguish from the turmoil of the water, stirred and reshuffled in a seething lava-like mass. Up above, the lamp of the lighthouse clattered out its sequence of whip strokes. Everything around them emanated tension and the obscure attraction people some-times feel for despair. The black of the sea was glossier than the night; varnished, insalubrious and tempting. Boris, who was not used to the area and knew nothing of its dangers, was not afraid of it.

He was exploring more than a new environment, it was a whole new universe, the panorama of an entire family, a universe in which no one really worries whether there will be a tomorrow, or about what they will do with it; a universe from which he knew he was excluded, to the point of envy and of anger, and yet he had a pathetic certainty that he had been made for it . . . He headed towards the water, unbuckling his belt and tossing an 'Are you coming, then?' to the others, like a challenge.

'Surely, you don't mean . . . ?'

The father was horrified to see his daughters following the man, convinced that the spot was not a good choice, that the sea was at its fiercest here. He protested about the currents, intoning dramatically about the wind, which could whip up in a matter of minutes . . . But he could hear them laughing, further and further away, even though he could not see them. Defeated, he told himself there was no point, and set off home, muttering under his breath, taking a path that he at least could claim to know by heart.

In the depths of the all-encompassing darkness, they stood at first with just their feet in the water, struck by the brutal contrast of temperature and knowing it would take an effort of will to grow accustomed to it. They initiated themselves into this darkness as it gradually encroached up to their knees, rose up along their thighs, ran between their legs then over their stomachs, and came as a shock when it reached their chests . . . It was then that Julie's hand sought out Boris's, providing enough extra courage to submerge themselves completely. In that shivering moment she reached for Vanessa's arm with her other hand, so as not to leave her out or exclude her from anything.

It was Boris who came up with the idea of trying to reach the Gulf Stream, about a hundred metres away, or possibly two hundred. By virtue of the fact that they thought it would be impossible, they started to follow him, as if this game might provide a substitute for boredom at last. They also felt a little twinge of apprehension, that feeling of having to rely on someone else without being really sure of them, without any real trust, perfectly aware that that was exactly what made it so pleasurable. Boris swam on ahead of them, faster and faster, as if trying to shake them off. He was already reduced to a gleaming sliver, a wake that melted into the water.

When Julie looked back she could make out nothing behind her, no more than she could see up ahead or peering into the depths, nothing tangible except for the stars, and Vanessa close by. She swallowed hard, taking in a little water at the same time, then gripped on to her sister, suddenly furious with this man (whom she was still, never-theless, trying to follow), this man she wanted to curse almost as much as she wanted to stay with him, this man she was going to have to swim to because, in fact, she was much more afraid of turning back than catching up with him.

Up ahead, he ploughed on stubbornly, as if ex-acting some kind of revenge, as if spinning out some intimate satisfaction, seeing just how far they would go. All he had to do was set off into the inky water and they would follow him – already. They trusted him that much – already. You never really tire of that sort of attitude.

Boris was feeding his fervour to open himself up to danger, his need to throw the windows open to the storm, to push things to their limits – people as well as situations, motorbikes as well as ideas, and mistakes too, just to see. But he did stop. In the silent lapping of the water, hanging in the bottomless darkness, he waited for them to reach him, anticipating the shameless abandon of those two naked bodies gliding towards him.

There is a certain pathos in that pink granite coast-line, in the application with which the rock erodes so irregularly, in places bearing all the jagged mutilations of an accident, as if the waves driven to break here were the victims of some impact, as if they constituted a series of collisions . . . unless it is the rock itself that suffers, tortured for no good reason and from the beginning of time, until it gives way at last, until one day the island is completely conquered and finally dissolves.

As soon as the sun goes in, as soon as the wind turns and becomes unfavourable, the waters begin to look like a raging maelstrom, a scribbled turmoil fulminating up to the horizon. The shoreline becomes insane, lifting great handfuls of wanton waves, waves resigned to collapse at their journey's end, but not before tasting their revenge. Sailors are wary of the area, treating it like a maze dotted with traps. When the sea draws out at low tide, the treacherous reefs loom against the night, the bay empties itself as if suffering the effects of a purgative, and in this debacle it sucks up currents more violent than a mountain torrent. Then in an instant the sea swings back, drawn to the gaping space, galloping in the opposite direction, covering whole stretches of shoreline on the days of its greatest momentum, flooding ports as well as boats, scattering a few stragglers on the beach, and turning back again all the more forcefully afterwards, hauling its booty out and dropping it far from the shore, a payback for the leisure activities it grudgingly grants.

That is why many of the rocks in the area bear a cross, why the depths are haunted by the shipwrecks of other lives.

The policeman stood at the bow. The launch was empty that morning, and its progress was the less laboured for it. This was partly because it was too early for there to be many people around, but also, given the weather, they were more likely to be thinking of having a lie-in than going for a swim. There were just a few shreds of the overnight storm left in the exhausted sky, the residues of a few cold clouds, which would soon have put up the last of their resistance. The storm had started up late in the night, at about two o'clock in the morning, and had strung itself out, dripping on until dawn. A few old rumbles of thunder still rolled around in the distance, the muffled sounds of defeat, like a party being dismantled. Coming towards it, navigating over to it like that, the island looked absolutely deserted that morning, worn out by the night it had spent.

The policeman replied half-heartedly to the captain who insisted on asking him endless questions, repeating each one to make himself heard above the noise. He wanted to know more about the body that had been found that morning, because the more he knew the more he would be able to tell everyone else, once they all started talking about it.

Although he did not remain entirely impenetrable, the policeman was careful not to say too much in reply, after all, this sort of thing was just routine to him. With the combination of boats, inlets and holidaymakers, all it took was a storm on top of a slightly higher tide and it was the same story every year, the sea always took its dues; except that they were usually notified that someone was missing before the body was found.

'Which makes you think that in this case no one really gave a damn . . .'

At nearly ten o'clock the household was still fast asleep. Outside a lifeless chill reigned, as if the heat of the previous day had never existed, already a distant memory. The fine mist drizzled an overwhelming sense of pessimism over the coast, many people were struck by a feeling that it was all over, that the sun would never come back and the sea would sulk indefinitely, leaving the holiday season in ruins, swept away – definitively. They even missed all the noise and hubbub of the previous day on the beach, the cries and the crowds, which were in fact a necessary corollary of good weather.

'Don't worry, it changes quickly here . . . you'll see, by midday it'll be so hot it'll be unbearable.'

The father had been up a long time. He was there to greet Boris in the kitchen, to put his coffee into the microwave to heat up, and to show him how the toaster worked.

'I hope you won't hold it against me for abandoning you last night, but I felt happier coming home. I'm a bit old for midnight swims, you know, the sea's a bit of a shock to my system in broad daylight . . . And, anyway, I could see that the three of you were getting along fine.'

The toaster punctuated the silence.

'Your toast's ready. Still, I hope you'll believe me when I tell you that, in my day, I wasn't backward in coming forward for a midnight swim, sometimes I'd even make it out to those little islands right up to the north, rather tempting fate . . . By the way, I haven't seen Julie this morning, have you?'

Boris felt the question bearing down on him like a wave of hidden meaning. It was inevitable, they were bound to ask him.

'She usually wakes up before everyone else, but when I knocked on her door this morning there was no reply. I didn't knock again . . . I think your coffee'll be hot now.'

Boris burned himself so badly taking his coffee from the microwave that he dropped the cup, instantly resenting the father for not warning him.

'It's my fault, I should have warned you. What do you expect? Those contraptions are as impenetrable to me as the great unanswered questions of the universe . . . twenty seconds to boil a mug of coffee, a real mystery. I don't know about you, but it's completely beyond me. Like particle accelerators and mapping the human genome, can you begin to grasp that sort of thing?'

Boris never wanted to sustain any degree of conversation first thing in the morning. On top of his usual morning mood he now had the pain of the burn shooting from the tips of his fingers. The best he could do was to blow on them, holding his right hand in his left, as if it were someone else's.

'People my age usually know all sorts of ways of dealing with burns: ice cubes or butter, or incantations even . . . Apart from the doctor's phone number, I don't really know anything. We've got a

60

friend on the other side of the island who's a doctor.'

Just for a moment Boris felt as if the father had deliberately set the microwave on high. The limitations of his morning mood.

The fact that someone knocked on the kitchen window added to the confusion. It was the policeman trying to catch their attention, almost regretting knocking so loudly. The father indicated that he would come out to see him, and asked his guest if he would excuse him . . . please, do make yourself at home.

There is always some embarrassment when you find yourself alone in other people's houses, an obscure feeling of awkwardness. Boris had never suffered from this unsettling feeling, in fact with him it was quite the contrary, he even derived some pleasure from opening an unfamiliar cupboard, discovering its particular configuration, seeing just beyond the permitted boundary. Through the wet panes he could make out the father, still in his dressing-gown, listening attentively to what the policeman was saying. The latter seemed deferential, perhaps even respectful perhaps towards this elderly man, as he stood there with his kepi under his arm. The father did not seem to be saying much to him, clearly perplexed, but at one point he did sign a document that the other man handed to him, he signed it with a rather grumpy flourish and then watched for a long while as the policeman made his way back towards the gate.

Still in his slippers, the father walked to the limits of the property, by the edge of the cliff, to a spot that overlooks the whole bay. He swept his eyes from one side to the other, inspecting the area, thoughtful, even rather serious. That was when Boris, still feeling quite at home, made himself a second cup of coffee, put another slice of bread in the toaster and adjusted the setting on the microwave. While he waited for it all to heat up he surveyed the kitchen, the swimming pool rippling just outside . . . going over it all in his mind, applying himself to the minimal effort required to imagine he was in his own home. When all is said and done, it is a real crime being in someone else's house and imagining oneself at home, it is a discreet form of offence, hard to detect, but quite satisfying in some cases, if you can just leave it at that.

At that exact moment she emerged, painfully, suffering, having such trouble recovering. She found it really difficult to get out of bed this morning, feeling a sense of refusal, her body aching but somehow soothed, as if she had suffered in some way, or had gone too far the night before. She had to surface from so deep down, not only because of the impression of water all around her, but also due to her total absence of energy, a lethal heaviness from swimming in the cold for too long.

But most of all there was him, this man whose every movement seemed to outstrip his intentions, whose arms had held her too tightly, the pain it had cost her resisting him, and – in spite of everything – his gentleness when he released her, the incomparable thrill of two bodies coming together . . .

They had guiltily camouflaged the sounds in the murmur of the waves, their fingers teetering on each other's lips, their lips greedily sucking the fingers, each action exacerbated by the restraint; but she very soon felt uneasy knowing her sister was so close by, a sudden scruple that made her uncomfortable, icy cold even, the disquiet as she sensed her coming closer . . .

That was when she felt that refusal would be the ultimate pleasure, escaping his hold on her, shaking off her desire and throwing herself back into the fluid waves, letting him get that far, so quickly and easily, and then leaving as if to disown him all the more emphatically.

That was also why she had slept in her room, and he in his. Despite the languor that always threatened to overwhelm her here, the feeling she was tanning herself for nothing, despite the fierce longing she felt to be with this providential man, she had not given in. She may well have been a little disappointed by his insistence, the urgency and persistence he had demonstrated once they were in the corridor, when she herself was worried about only one thing, not to appear too readily available. He had not insisted any further, had turned on his heel and walked to his room, not even piqued – and the more seductive for it. Which did not alter the fact that she had thought about him all night, all night she had gone over that borderline violence in her mind, until she even

64

longed for it. So that in the morning the only thing that really worried her, her only regret, was the uncomfortable feeling, the fear that someone might actually have heard them.

This was already the second trip for the captain. Navigating between the hump-backed waves and the outcrops of reef, respecting the channel while making allowances for the currents, passing as close as possible to one rock in order to skirt clear of another – it was all routine to him.

The ferry rocked gently between the landmarks, little crosses rusting on top of areas of reef to make them stand out more clearly. At high tide only the crucifixes emerged but at low tide they looked like tombs, empty soulless ones.

The sun had come back. In the powerful light and the renewed heat, André-Pierre was subjected to the scenery around him, but took no interest in it. The mother had been waiting for this moment for more than three weeks, she had been hoping for nothing else since the beginning of the holidays, to engineer an opportunity to corner him, to be alone with him. This morning she had used the excuse of all the shopping she had to do in Paimpol, mentioning the bottles of water and the baskets that would need carrying, to get him to go with her. She did not like going there alone anyway because of the rumours about a gang who busked and begged on the edge of the market, youngsters who hung around for the whole summer and who now rather frightened her, given all the stories there were about them claiming they were only there so that they could really watch you and learn all sorts of things about you with a view to knowing exactly when your house would be deserted, when you wouldn't be there.

In order to exonerate herself from these suspicions, and probably also as a way of courting them, the mother always granted them a gracious '*bonjour*', particularly as they were all boys, all smiles, which implied that she was still beautiful, plenty of them might even have been prepared to get involved with this grandmother.

As well as replenishing supplies, today's trip was an opportunity for her to clear up two or three things with her son-in-law. She had always found it terribly difficult to communicate with him, which did not mean she could not love him, or take him on unreservedly. In any event, mothers – even the least maternal – are never completely hostile towards their sons-in-law, in some cases they are even grateful to them, all the more so when they know just what a bad start their daughters got off to in life.

When André-Pierre met Vanessa she had not yet escaped the protracted disaster that was her adolescence, a succession of events that had propelled her into adulthood without any kind of diploma, with no stability or plans, nothing but some bad acquaintances and a chronic state of despair; you could be forgiven for thinking that, while he was at it, her brother had done his best to copy her. Like many others, Vanessa had thought it her duty to express herself by rebelling, but true protest requires at least the courage to formulate it, a degree of commitment: she had opted for a more intimate form of rebellion, a more muffled nihilism. Which meant that, after endless phases spent in various cities and – allegedly – at university, she had stayed in the bosom of her family, doing precious little, half-heartedly helping out with the Estate, as a temporary employee. At one stage her father had tried to make her a representative, a sort of ambassador for his business, in fact she was the one who had had the idea of doing up special rooms for wine-tastings, decorating them and fitting them with a public address system. So that, in this context, it was quite natural that André-Pierre should make himself noticed. André-Pierre who had been working for the Estate for a long time, who had risen from the level of financial director to managing director in the space of a few years, André-Pierre who – even before he started seeing the daughter of the Estate – already rejoiced in the father's unfailing trust, taking over from him during holidays, compensating for his increasing lack of interest in the business . . . André-Pierre who had even managed to conquer Japan because he was not afraid of the return trips by aeroplane, André-Pierre who, at the end of the day, gave Vanessa every semblance of being a woman as well as a double dose of motherhood. It was quite clear that this particular André-Pierre, who had started out merely as a brilliant colleague, a sensible creature whom everyone liked well enough (but no more than that, precisely because he was too sensible), it was quite clear that when he had become part of the family everyone had learned to like him a little better.

When it came down to it, there was only André-Pierre to ensure the company's future, on the condition, however, that he consented to share the responsibilities with Philip at some stage, because the father had still not given up on a possible capitulation on his son's part, and saw him as the only hope of continuing the male line and the family name. In view of the son's imminent installation at the controls of the company, it was vital that the two men saw eye to eye: the father, who was pinning his hopes on this two-man partnership, did not under any circumstances want to hear of differences of opinion or hostility between them.

Now over seventy-five, he deemed that his share of the work had been done, and he – and, indeed, his wife – longed for only one thing: to spend as much time as possible here at Bréhat, and not have to worry about anything any more.

'But you know Philip, he'll never change; deep down people never change . . . and just sitting him at a nice desk and giving him some shares and a job to do won't suddenly make him grow up.'

'You know, André-Pierre, since you've been one of the family I've loved you as much as my own children, I care about you just as much, but in exchange it falls on you to love them too, and therefore to help them. It is up to you to keep an eye on Philip. I do realize that in the early days you'll have to be – I was going to say like a father to him – but let's say like a brother . . . You must understand that it's important, both to him and to us, and that he can't carry on without work indefinitely, traipsing round the world like this his whole life . . .'

It was at this stage that André-Pierre revealed his true character (a character capable of sulking profoundly), as he turned away coolly and gazed at the sequence of rusted crosses, perhaps seeing them as a procession of trophies, examples of the peculiar sense of superiority some derive from marking out where others have failed – a self-righteous attitude that held no appeal to him. And the stony expression on his face, the uncompromising stance (which had the one advantage of simplifying everything), was cobbled together out of pure egotism, a selfishness that spared him any feelings of compassion . . . Philip – he could hardly even see him as a salesman, a rep, he might just about be able to help out with the vines, putting in new stakes, spreading the sulphate . . . André-Pierre knew his brother-in-law too well to underestimate just how inconsequential he was, especially as he (unlike all the others) knew about all his escapades and strange set-ups. He had been protecting the family from them for a long time, keeping to himself the secrets and sordid goings-on that would almost certainly have altered the image they had of a prodigal son. They might not go so far as to disown him but there was no doubting they would see him in a different light . . . In fact, he was the last rampart of the son's respectability, and he expected some form of indemnity in return. André-Pierre harboured all Philip's entanglements, keeping them safe, a collection of irrefutable arguments. Until now he had never said anything about the money he gave to Philip every month, or the exact address to which he sent the mail, not to mention his crafty intervention to ensure that the postcards did indeed appear to be from the United States.

It could be that this sort of revelation would change nothing, the mother would find it in her to forgive him once again, the father would shrug it all off, absolving him out of principle. Particularly as it would not be the first time that André-Pierre had tried to discredit him, it even amounted to a sustained effort since right from the start he had realized just how difficult it would be to get on with the guy. As far as he was concerned, Philip was a definitive waster, a total incompetent whose only experience was his aimless wandering punctuated by petty trafficking and dubious acquaintances.

'. . . You only have to look at who his friends are, like this guy at the house now. Can't you see that he's already made himself at home after just two days? Haven't you seen the way he wanders about with his hashish, making everybody smoke the stuff . . . ?'

'You must be the only person I know who still takes offence at that.'

'But can't you see that if we let him get away with it, it won't be long before the guy's taking the shirts off our backs, perhaps even—'

With these words he stopped abruptly, as if

afraid that somehow, wherever he might be – and in some almost supernatural way – Boris might hear him . . .

'You shouldn't take against people like that. He's a charming boy. He and my husband chatted for ages last night and, believe me, my husband knows a good deal about character.'

André-Pierre knew every reason why he should be wary of this man, should hate him, convinced that everything about him was false, designed to entice, so much so in fact that he could not picture him anywhere else except beside the sea, he could not imagine him in any place other than here, enjoying other people's sunshine, dispensing his beady glances, a sort of parasite you could say, and one completely devoid of class . . . Compared to him, even Philip seemed to have some breeding. He did not for one minute believe this show-off had been through Buzenval, not for one minute could he imagine him at the Lasalliens, those sorts of places do imprint a modicum of polish on those who go through them, a suggestion of good manners, however small . . .

'And how come you've never met him before?'

'What little free time children have at boarding-school is not spent going to stay with other people's parents . . . and, anyway, Philip never brought a single friend home, I think it was mainly because he felt guilty for being so well-off, when I think a lot of children in his shoes would have done exactly the opposite.'

Once again André-Pierre turned away, clenching his teeth to stop himself from speaking, gazing vacantly over the futile waves.

'Come on, come on now, I know you're under a lot of pressure at the moment, that you're working long hours, but please don't worry, take it from me, my husband and I have complete faith in you . . . I'm sure you're going to deal with it brilliantly, I'm quite sure, but you have to understand that I would still like to ask one thing of you, let's call it a favour: make peace with Philip. In fact, this would be a perfect opportunity for the two of you to talk – it's the holidays, there's no better time for straightening things out . . . I'm asking you to do this for my sake, he's got everything he needs here, I don't want him to be in the States any longer, there's nothing for him there.'

Confronted with the full extent of her gullibility . . . that was when he really had to clench his teeth.

The ferry skimmed along more quickly now. The captain had relit his faltering Players cigarette, a sure sign that they had passed the difficult currents, that he no longer had to compensate for the drift by holding firmly to the helm. His smoke hung in the cabin for a while, protected from the wind, spiralling above him, thick and yellow, then – straying just a little too far – it suddenly disappeared, dispersing outside instantly, instantly swallowed up.

Slumbering directly underneath them, concealed under four or five metres of water, was the pathway out to the island known as the *Lady's Thigh*, the footsteps through it erased by the tide, clues swallowed up by the ocean, a path that – just a few hours ago – had still been open to the air, and would be again a little later.

When Julie came down from her room Boris and the father were by the pool. With her hand raised to shield her eyes from the sun, she kissed her father and mumbled a quiet hello to Boris. She said she had seen the policeman this morning, through her window, a disturbing sight first thing . . . The father reassured her with a laugh, a bright flash of laughter, one of those surges of derision conferred, in all their subtlety, by the wisdom of age, and which vouch for the relativity of all things. A child's laugh is, after all, only ever the laugh of someone who knows nothing, a laugh that has yet to appreciate the scale that ranges from the calamitous to the casual, from the anecdotal to the essential; the laugh of an elderly man is exactly the opposite . . . the father's laugh was a blast of perceptiveness, brushing everything aside, a laugh that dismissed Julie, as if she were a child, glad she had nothing to worry about. She buried her dreamy expression in her bowl of coffee, darting still-sleepy glances over the rim, then she took a deep breath and re-established contact with the great expanse of sky, the triumphant sunlight and the sea, which was blue once again, playing its modulations around the pink granite.

'But, all the same,' said the father, 'don't talk about it, especially not to your mother. This time he wanted me to sign some sort of permission form about the fireworks, the most officious piece of paper . . .'

Then, turning to Boris: 'Last year, unfortunately, one of the rockets set fire to two yachts anchored below the house, in White Hen Bay. Actually, we've been worrying ever since that the owners would make some sort of reprisals. What do you expect? Philip had had a bit to drink . . . Well, I expect he told you all about it.'

Now, though, he was no longer joking.

Vanessa and the children came up from the inlet, with two little yellow buckets full of shells, and their oilskins over their arms; they had been gone more than two hours.

They had lunch in the downstairs sitting room, in the cool, with the shutters half closed. A woman came at midday to prepare the meal and then to serve it. Boris watched the ageless creature's comings and goings as she went from the kitchen to the table, her every movement intended to improve the meal. When all was said and done, she was the only one he could not really pin down: did she live here, did she come from the mainland, what did her voice sound like when she was not careful how she spoke? Watching her from behind as she moved away, he could picture her mother . . . who worked in a restaurant, he was quite sure of that.

The father held everyone's attention by repeating an anecdote the policeman had passed on to him that morning, and which was probably doing the rounds of the island at that very moment (people like nothing better than picking over someone else's death). A man had been fished out of the sea at dawn, trapped in the sanctuary provided by the rocks that surrounded the island, like the poor chap two years before. The father himself attributed these accidents to the hare-brained ideas some cranks had when they were out swimming. The challenge amongst them was to swim out and join the Gulf Stream, preferably at low tide, when it was as close as possible, and then they would just let themselves be carried by the warm waters . . .

'A few years ago that sort of parody of heroism was very fashionable, they were disciples of Ponce de Leon, in a manner of speaking, he was the injured conquistador whose body was brought home by the current. Legend has it that the Gulf Stream carried him all the way here, opening up the way for anyone who planned to emigrate from America at no expense . . . Don't go thinking that it's just a legend, remember that white sharks really do let the Gulf Stream carry them to avoid the exertion of swimming, and as for the eels that are fished locally, most of them hatched in the Sargasso Sea . . . I personally see something of a metaphor in it. It could even be that that's how Philip will come back to us . . .'

The father had sown the seeds of disquiet once again. They all paused to work out whether this was humorous or just bad taste.

'Mind you, if he's going to choose the Gulf Stream instead of an aeroplane, we won't be seeing him for a couple of months . . .'

Only Boris laughed at this. The father was delighted to find someone who was a match for him, at last there was someone round this table who could take these things lightly, who would not suffer at the hands of every little joke, the others were all inclined to take things at face value . . .

Boris's complicity restored a little of the patri-arch's credibility. Recently they had all been increasingly inclined to think of him as a bit of a dreamer, if not a cynical fabulator . . . André-Pierre did not savour this new complicity, afraid that within it lay the beginnings of future collaboration.

As she listened, Julie thought of their swim the previous night.

'But this Gulf Stream, how would you know you'd found it?'

'It's like a river, right in the middle of the sea, a river with banks of sea water.'

'And to get to it?'

'You just have to follow the flying fish . . .'

The woman with the dishes no longer minded that most of what they said and did was completely alien to her; she had grown used to it.

*   *   *

80

That afternoon the girls suggested they should all go to the tennis courts, particularly as tennis was the major sporting activity at Buzenval. Tournaments filled up entire weekends for all the boarders, which was why Philip excelled at the game, and why Boris should be pretty good. André-Pierre did not try to wriggle out of it, he would not have had a clear conscience, he could anticipate how they would have gone on and on at him about it.

Up in his room, the father was thinking rather more than taking his siesta, daydreaming about drifting waters, all the different movements of the warm currents that made the summers here so blissful, a real microclimate, which meant that, as well as the palm trees and umbrella pines, even eucalyptuses and mangroves grew here. He would often fall asleep with a particular image, an attempt to picture this thing that had always obsessed him, even though to that day, he had never truly been able to visualize it: fifty times more than the Loire . . . The Gulf Stream shifts fifty times more water than the Loire, that godsend of a river that had made his fortune as well as his wines . . . He concentrated on that until he was overtaken by sleep, with sheep in the shape of white sharks.

The court was set back in the grounds, in a little clearing well sheltered from the wind. You reached it along a narrow path of beaten earth, a sinuous thread of saffron twisting between the pine trees. The warm, balsamic smell similar to Mediterranean scrubland, the high-summer heat, the languid way the girls moved, the weight of every shred of clothing – everything conjured up the Riviera. Especially as at that time of day the sun beat down with all its force. The tree bark was almost red, the clusters of pine needles blazed like volleys of emeralds, the sky stretched out its freshly painted hues as a backdrop. Through the gaps in the trees the sea sparkled, a second dimension of the same mirage. There, in the middle of that Grecian blue, the island seemed to be suspended between the sky and the sea, apparently above the water, just skimming the sky. Boris stepped into this scene as if into a fairytale, slightly incredulous to find himself here, being careful to walk steadily to reveal nothing of the appalling contrast he was experiencing in relation to the last few months . . .

It was as he turned a corner round the tall trees that he came across the high wire-netting fence that ran all the way round the court, high enough to make him feel dizzy, as abrasive as his worst memories of being outdoors, those walks he had taken when the horizon was criss-crossed with steel mesh. This netting in front of him was more forgiving, it enclosed nothing more than a little patch of freedom, reached through an unlocked door; but still, when he saw it, he felt an almost physical blow, so that he faltered internally, so that he folded, but knew he must betray absolutely nothing.

The girls decided they would wait for the heat to subside; they would stay on the bench and watch the men rather than playing doubles.

As well as the shock of the netting, Boris felt an accumulation of remembered humiliations flooding back, more disabling than an Achilles' heel. Tennis: it was just a sport after all, but to him it was so emblematic, so humiliating . . . It was that unbearable air of superiority others assumed as soon as they took out the yellow balls, the rackets and the white shorts. They had done nothing to deserve this supremacy, there was no reason why they should be more adept. Bare-fisted, they certainly would not have had any advantage, but with a racket in their hands a particular quality in them re-asserted its rights, a facility for gliding over the court, a form of upbringing revealed itself . . . Even so, however much he dreaded this particular test, he had never shrunk from it; each time he had been asked whether he would like to play, he had played, convinced that – by substituting instinct for rules, and furious determination for convention – he could win here too.

'Apparently, there were two tournaments a year at Buzenval.' You must have won it every time, didn't you?'

If André-Pierre was indulging in irony right from the start, if he was eyeing his opponent contemptuously before they had even started to play, it was because he could see just how ill at ease Boris was with his racket, something in the way he moved was not quite right, he had lost some of his insolent fluidity, and even looked ungainly.

Boris had authoritatively designated who should be at which end, putting André-Pierre facing the full glare of the sun, but before the game even began André-Pierre asked for a pause to have a drink. Boris tried one last time to persuade the girls to play doubles, claiming that it would be so much more fun if all four of them were on court, but they did not want to. Sitting in the shade with their feet up on the bench, they were happier watching; they thought it was more fun.

Just seeing them there put extra pressure on him. Julie had her legs in the sun, the rest of her body back in the shade. From where he stood Boris gazed at length at those thighs offered like that, quavering in the face of her brazen exhibitionism as she looked him straight in the eye. Vanessa watched this little performance, feeling neither jealousy nor offence, just a touch of resigned complicity . . .

'Come on then, let's get on with it . . .' André-Pierre sparked very energetically, hopping from foot to foot, facing his opponent with just a hint of defiance.

'All right, but we'll knock up a bit first . . .'

They sent each other a dozen or so trial shots, one by one Boris sent them outside the lines, and he was already thirsty, already hot. Shielding his eyes from the sun with his hand, André-Pierre watched him, annoyed to have to break off so soon. Boris suddenly made the dishonest claim that he would rather be at the other end, having thought about it, he would rather play facing the sun . . . André-Pierre should have seen this gesture as a consideration, a thoughtful concern, but he was trying to look beneath the suggestion, to spot the trap.

*   *   *

As she prepared Philip's bedroom, the mother rummaged through the mess that always slumbered there, a sort of archive of her son that she had never had the nostalgia or the indiscretion to dig through. She exhumed piles of old homework from the cupboard, a succession of books that featured more scribbling and doodling than notes taken about lessons; and always, whatever the homework was, always bad marks . . . She also found a number of notes that she herself should have written in her time, but it was someone else who had actually signed them . . . she had known all about this particular talent of her son's, this ability to copy other people's signatures, and the nerve for doing that sort of thing; they were crimes really, and he had been committing them from such a young age . . . In fact, for a long time she had worried that, with such aptitudes and sang-froid, her son's true vocation would be nothing other than dissimulation and lies, she had been afraid of this tendency of his for some time. Hence the boarding-school. Hence the need for such discipline, the sort of establishment from which he should have emerged utterly subdued, honest to the core.

She would have preferred to find a proper class photograph, something really organized with a list of all the names corresponding to the faces, below or to one side, making it easy to find the one you were looking for, whereas this was just a shot of the choir, the choir in its entirety, granted, some fifty pupils, but without the names. She did not have her glasses but that did not stop her recognizing her son straight away, her son in his alb, just like all the others, with their strings of wooden rosary beads around their necks, their close-cropped hair, proper little gentlemen, and with that extra-ordinarily upright posture, almost proud (as if Philip ever felt the slightest hint of pride wearing that sort of outfit!). In fact, it made her laugh seeing Philip in that light, Philip with short hair and the determined little face of a schoolboy resolved to do what was right, a Philip who seemed appeased, sanctified, and all in white too . . .

The others were also standing very upright, five rows of perfect specimens, like seed trays, a breeding ground for excellence . . . But the one she was actually looking for was a tall boy, this Boris who, if she remembered correctly, must have spent a lot of time in detention with her son, in-separable, so much so that they probably had to split them up at one stage, to put them in different classes for a while . . . At a rather more crucial period in their adolescence there had even been the business of practical jokes, sort of traps that a handful of pupils set for some of the others, real ambushes in which they beat their victims with conscientious thoroughness, launching into horrifying violence without any explanation, without anyone really knowing why . . . Following this episode, it was a question of sanctions and consultations with psychologists. Philip featured in that handful of individuals, but he had always maintained that he had only followed the others: being part of the gang that dispensed the blows had been the best option for avoiding them yourself. His only part in the whole business had been to watch, which did not alter the fact that he had been diagnosed as being violently argumentative with an indubitable tendency to aggressive behaviour . . . When all's said and done, it was the sort of thing that happens in all boarding-schools, violence that's been allowed to ferment for too long, you get it in prisons too, tensions created by the boys' resentment at being there at all, knowing that they can't get out.

The more she applied herself to the photograph, the more she pored over it, the more difficulty she had in seeing clearly along those rows of perfectly pathetic little angels. And yet some of them did have that solid, soldier-like bearing that Boris already had at the time, but then which one was he exactly . . . She did not have her glasses, but she went on stubbornly looking for one with the right build, those features that managed to be fine as well as quite pronounced, that crew-cut hair and those dark eyes, an adolescent who must have shown some of the sparkle of the man he was now . . . She skimmed through the lower rows before realizing that, given his height, he was more likely to be further up. So she slid her eye over the faces a little longer, until they all looked the same, always in the same garb, with the same pallor scalding her eyes . . .

Determined to study the thing more closely, she took the photograph downstairs with her.

Before leaving, she closed the shutters – anything to keep the room cool. She dusted down the bed for the umpteenth time and scanned the room once more, she wanted it all to be perfect.

Down below, the siesta was over. *Casta diva* was building up the barcarole of its opening chords; one by one the shutters spilled delight back into the room. The mother sang along to herself, as if she had not tired of hearing it, at the same time every day, just as she was always gratified to discern signs of impatience from the children's bedroom. At their age you only have to cry to make yourself understood.

When they saw her coming, they whooped a triumphant *Granny!* . . . Overwhelmed by their little reddened faces, delighting in the cheeky toddlers as she held them in her arms and they wriggled and twitched like two nets full of fish, she forgot the photograph and took the two little creatures downstairs to unleash them back into real life. It was such a pleasure rediscovering her maternal concerns, the mixture of anxiety and satisfaction that comes with looking after two boys. Her husband also enjoyed the novelty of playing at being a grandfather, although not for too long.

Now he was no longer striking with just his arm. Now he was putting more than his strength into it, there was anger too . . . Everything was wrong now, the sun right in his line of vision, the sweat burning his eyes, the fury at being confronted once again with this ridiculous game, this impossible game, which he was no good at, which always saw him fail.

In fact, the game had been reduced to this, André-Pierre watching the balls pelting towards him, mad and murderous, some of them in, most of them out, not to mention the ones that smacked straight into him . . . Boris concluded every rally by hitting the ball too hard, aiming haphazardly but hard. They felt like warning shots to André-Pierre, these balls hurtling towards every part of his body, balls he took as signs of malicious intent, as disturbing as someone telephoning and hanging up on you in the middle of the night . . .

Seeing that the sun was obviously upsetting his

opponent, André-Pierre suggested they changed ends.

'It wouldn't make any difference,' Boris retorted tartly, making the most of this brief lapse in concentration to send him the fastest ball imaginable, a gunshot more than a service . . .

And that vitriolic glance every time, just before starting play, the venomous way Boris had of asking whether he was ready . . . There may even have been a couple of insults in those grunts that come out with a powerful serve, the odd *aaaa-sole* or a *y're dead* . . . What was more, instead of apologizing when the ball went miles out, instead of saying nothing or pretending to be annoyed with himself, Boris – who had become excessively familiar – showered him with remonstrances as if dealing with a child: 'Well, get on with it, you've got to run . . . go on, go for it, my man, you can get that one, go on . . .'

The man's mad! André-Pierre kept telling himself, as if this had become his creed. The guy's completely sick . . . At the same time he made sure he addressed every shot with application, trying not to lose his concentration, because this was certainly exactly what Boris was hoping for, to unsettle him . . .

Knowing that spite and anger were not options, and aware that no riposte from him could counter so much bad faith, instead of responding in kind or taking offence, André-Pierre chose cowardice, the last resort for pride; cowardice that salvages the worst situations just as surely as courage. The girls were strolling through the pine trees, sharing one of those cigarettes that the other guy must have rolled; he watched them helplessly from a distance, inwardly begging for them to come back over by the court because, since they had stopped watching, the other had let himself go even more, he was making the most of the fact that there were no witnesses to display the full extent of his violence and bad faith . . . Just then Boris hurled him a devastating service, even though his feet were well over the line, and awarded himself the point without any scruples . . .

'Careful, I'm coming back at you . . . forty – fifteen!'

The guy's mad! He was now quite sure of it, you just had to play tennis against him to realize he was . . . The man's sick, he can't be here just by chance, he's not here simply to lose at tennis and to set the women all aquiver . . . Singled out as the target of his penetrating glare, paralysed by the profound acuity of his resentment, André-Pierre even began to wonder whether Boris was here for him, perhaps nothing else was of any interest to him, just this brother-in-law who was so annoying, so unsympathetic, this brother-in-law who was so clearly in the way, and who could actually be neutralized quite easily, just with a bit of aggression and intimidation . . .

He felt his sweat flow more profusely. Now he was the one losing point after point. Now he was not in the match at all, half paralysed by this pernicious intuition, now he could only lumber awkwardly around the court as if the soles of his shoes were holding him back, a leaden sensation that weighed down his arms and dampened his returns. It was years since he had felt like this, the first signs of a proper attack of tetany, now even the easy shots were getting away, his racket had become limp and the net was too high, and most of all he was aware of his frantic expression, the dazed way he watched his opponent, incredulous if not actually afraid, when in fact he was terrified . . . This time he was not suffering from minor anxieties and suspicions, but full-blown certainties. He was no longer exploring assumptions, but already concentrating on how to escape the situation. What was he waiting for then? And how was he going to go about it? Was he going to have to keep an eye on this guy the whole time, making sure he was never alone with him, avoiding him? Perhaps he should tell the father everything, even if it made him look like a coward, a chicken, a weakling; or dump him on the police, but on what grounds? What crime could you pin on him other than the brazen way he had frightened him and cheated at tennis? Or he could pre-empt him, tackle him head-on and ask him what he wanted, even giving him whatever it would take to get him to clear off . . . No doubt about it, Boris was the sort to hold out for the highest bidder, and if Philip had commissioned him, then his means would only stretch so far . . . So it was up to him to do it, to deflect this man who had been trained on him like a weapon.

He would never have believed he would one day have to contemplate something like this. He would never have believed this sort of situation could ever involve him, the whole scenario was like some tawdry piece of local news, just as disgusting, just as inconceivable, the sort of extreme set-up where people are such a burden that you can't help thinking about getting rid of them, of getting them off your back at any price . . . He kept hoping to hear that little voice inside his head, a discreet, disembodied little voice that spoke to him as if he were a child, the only thing that could comfort him.

It was on an apparently anodyne return of serve that André-Pierre exploded, bombarded by the balls, liquefied by his fears, he literally seemed to come unscrewed on the spot: his racket suddenly started spinning round him, and – on the other end of the handle – his body reeled after it, absorbed in this ironic spiralling, before collapsing with a heavy inanimate thud.

Boris jumped over the net so quickly that you could have been forgiven for thinking he was genuinely concerned. When they saw this, the girls realized something was going on and they ran over too. Boris was already cradling André-Pierre's head, he was already asking him what was wrong, he even thought to check that he was not swallowing his own tongue, before lifting his head back up and holding him like that. The girls unbuttoned his shirt and took off his sweat bands, and wiped his face with a towel.

He came back to his senses in Boris's arms and recoiled slightly, even though he could not actually move, gripped by the paralysing cramps . . .

'Tell me then, old man, aren't you glad I was playing facing the sun? You see, I *was* right to make you change ends, I know all about sun stroke . . .'

The girls said they would go and get a bottle of cold water from the house, a flannel, some aspirin and plenty of ice . . . André-Pierre tried to keep them there, he desperately wanted them not to leave, he desperately did not want to be left alone with this man . . . but he hardly had the strength to speak.

Boris continued to hold him up, not at all comfortable in his role as a nurse, moving as little as possible, gentle as can be. He even smoothed his hand over the other man's forehead, saying softly, 'Come on, AP, you're going to be fine, don't worry . . .'

André-Pierre was trying to speak, André-Pierre was struggling, André-Pierre who wanted at least to find the inner strength to tell him to piss off and leave him alone, André-Pierre who droned on inwardly – like a child who no longer even has the energy, like a child who already knows no one's going to listen to him, no one at all – André-Pierre who kept on repeating his obsessive complaint inside his head, despairingly, set to the rhythm of the pounding in his chest: *Why's he calling me AP? I don't want him to call me AP . . .*

The most offensive thing about people who have so much is their aptitude for neglect, their facility for contempt (to the extent that sometimes they no longer even know what they do have) . . . Pianos sleeping in hushed sitting rooms, paintings by minor masters shrouded in dust, treasures in attics, a great variety of curios . . . All his life Boris had sensed the extravagance of this kind of negligence.

The boathouse was built directly into the rock; a big, rusted iron door opened on to the creek to reveal the storage area littered with all sorts of boat fittings, rusting tools and torn old sails. The father was quite determined to show him the Riva, an Aquarama that dated from the seventies; he was even relying on Boris to get it started, you never know. Even though it had not been taken out for two years, he claimed you'd only have to dust off the spark plugs and flick the starter for the thing to fire up again straight away.

The father talked Boris through how to get her on to the water, a very simple procedure but one that did involve vigorously hauling on the winch and using your arms to manoeuvre the hull. The father watched Boris doing it with a sense of nostalgia for his own lost strength, perfectly charmed by the man's docility, perfectly overcome by his obliging cooperation; with him he was discovering a complicity he had never even felt with his own son . . . Mind you, perhaps the boy felt beholden to him, thought he owed him something for his hospitality. Perhaps he was forcing himself to be helpful, when he actually loathed dirtying his hands with grease and dragging out this mahogany relic . . . Particularly as, once the spark plugs and the distributor had been overhauled, it still did not work. Boris noticed – with stupefaction if not disgust – that the key was still on the dashboard, which meant it must have been there all that time, and no one had ever bothered to do anything about it, or even worried that someone might pinch the boat . . .

'Look, I don't want to bother you with this . . . Just leave it, it doesn't matter . . .'

Boris countered this with a stubborn insistence on continuing, a determination that surprised the father.

'I only really wanted to see if it would still turn

over, don't go wasting your time for nothing, and don't go and get yourself dirty, if nothing else I could get a mechanic to come over from the dockyard.'

'Just you wait and see, a couple more minutes and it'll be working . . .'

The father's face beamed all the more expansively. He was bemused by this determination, particularly as he did not really have any intention of using the Riva, he could not see himself climbing in and taking the controls, even if the idea was rather appealing . . .

'Actually, come to think of it, you might have a boat licence yourself?'

Boris lied by saying he had. Well, he had handled speedboats, always other people's, but probably deriving a thousand times more enjoyment from them than their owners would have done.

After several attempts to start it, each as fruitless as the last, Boris came and sat down next to the father without a word; both deeply disappointed. Then they simply sat there looking at the gently gleaming hull, the fixtures in chrome and brass that were so obstinately pleasing, the long seats with their cracked, peeling leather in a smart racing green, still chic in spite of everything . . . Even in this sorry state, even without the thrum of the eight-cylinder engine, the Riva looked valuable.

Despite the neglect that had seen it deteriorate, despite the dirt and the dents interrupting its smooth lines, it was still a real marvel that swayed before them, rocked by the gentle movement of the water, as if it knew it was being watched, as if it were trying to entice them . . . Boris could see the images of a nostalgia he had never had, he could picture the holidays they must have spent on board, the father thirty years younger, the girls in short white socks, the hours of water-skiing and the impromptu picnics wherever they happened to land amongst the islands . . . and Philip right in the middle of the picture, a nasty kid already contaminated by the fact that everything was so easy for him, by the luxury that was already setting him apart, giving him apparent power that people would later come to re-evaluate, even coming to see him as pathetic, a loser . . . It was almost a form of revenge for Boris to see the boat in such a state, it gave him a chance to compensate for his own holiday memories, the summers he had spent in a very different kind of picture, long periods of life spent foiling boredom . . . Being able to drive this little gem would redress the balance a bit.

'Do you know something – I'm telling you this because I know you're the reliable type – but it was me who asked the police to come over this morning . . . The body they found this morning was a man who'd tried to get out to the island on foot along

101

the *Lady's Thigh*, it's a passage you can follow at low tide, but only an initiated few know the way, and, to be honest, at one point I started wondering whether by any chance it could be . . .'

Boris laid his hand firmly on the old man's thigh.

'Come on . . . And, anyway, you know he's a very good swimmer.'

'Perhaps, but in the middle of the night . . . You see, the ferries don't run after eight o'clock, there isn't any choice . . . And you know what he's like in the evening, you couldn't say he goes without a drink . . .'

'But he would have rung to say he was in the area.'

'Philip's not the type to bother with formalities.'

'If it had come to that he would have found a fisherman or yachtsman who would drop him off.'

'Yes, probably . . . Let's just say it did cross my mind, but keep it to yourself.'

Boris rubbed his hands together vigorously to get rid of the engine oil, and he started rummaging through his trouser pockets. As he did, the father noticed that the white was decidedly less perfect than the day before, decidedly less immaculate, the seats of the Riva certainly had sullied him as he knelt to tinker with the engine . . .

The engine had definitely had it. The father saw it as a metaphor for his own vigour, the lack of drive and desire that made him drift gradually to the water's edge, no longer hurtling through the waves, like an old speedboat careened on the shore . . .

Because his trousers were so tight, Boris really had to push to slip his hand into his pocket. He took out a packet of cigarettes that had been completely crushed, and parked one in his mouth as he stood thoughtfully. The father declined the one he offered him, saying absently that he had not smoked for twenty years, but he did leap to his feet when he heard the match . . . He blew at Boris's fingers, pointing at all the jerrycans around them, all that petrol that neither of them had thought of . . . that was when they both burst out laughing. Such relief.

As he lay recuperating in the half-light of the sitting room, André-Pierre was ashen, weighed down by this strange feeling that would not pass. He had always been prone to bouts of tetany, the sort of condition that a man hardly likes to admit to, particularly as he had not suffered from it for nearly fifteen years. It was just as he was finishing his studies, in fact, at a time when he had felt furiously vulnerable – because that is where tetany strikes, right at the heart of someone who wavers, chilling their every fibre while they are disarmed, knocking them down just as they try to defend themselves . . . He was beginning to think that the worst enemy often lies within ourselves, that he could not think of a worse one, and that it might well be that he had no others.

The mother was the only one who seemed to show any interest in his predicament, at least she was the one who played nurse, staying by his side, administering aspirin, dabbing an ice-cold flannel over his forehead . . . He was painfully aware of the utter mediocrity of his position, particularly as the incident seemed to have had no effect on the others, it hadn't dampened the atmosphere that takes over a household the moment the sun beats down outside, while a pool ripples at the foot of the steps, and the sea twinkles close by . . . His wife, he could sense, was completely preoccupied with swimming and sunbathing, so he had appealed to the mother to stay with him, not to go too far away, abusing the indulgence that impressionable people show you when they know you are ill.

So there she was, excessively concerned and gentle, still not free of the reflex to take care of others.

'Can't you see that this man's weird? Haven't you noticed the way he hovers round Vanessa?'

'Well I never! you're jealous now . . . If she knew, I'm sure she'd be flattered . . .'

'I'm not joking, I mean do you really think it's normal that Philip hasn't arrived yet? What if he doesn't come? What if he's hiding, waiting for this other guy to do his business, or even . . . ?'

'What on earth are you talking about, my poor Pierre . . . ?'

'Or something could have happened to him . . .'

'Don't be ridiculous! Anyway, you know Philip . . . Do you remember last year? He only arrived on the morning of the fourteenth, and within a few

hours everything was set up, he set off his fireworks that same evening. Don't get so worked up,
you'll see, he'll be here tomorrow morning at worst
. . . He's a sensible boy at heart, you know that.
When it all comes down to it, he's always here
when he has to be. And that's what really matters,
don't you think?'

While André-Pierre was trying to get up (doing
nothing to exaggerate how difficult the process
was), there was something like an explosion
outside, a throaty gurgling of tubes followed by a
roaring that reverberated into an echo . . . He recognized the Riva's eight-cylinder engine firing up at
full throttle, shattering the air with its hoarse,
spluttering growl . . . The noise seemed to invade
the length of the coast, showering the whole area
with its supreme arrogance, what sort of idiot
could be revving it so hard, pumping on the
accelerator like machine-gun fire . . .

That man just kept on getting the upper hand . . .
André-Pierre let the sofa swallow him up again,
accepting as irrefutable the fact that this Boris – even
though he was a complete stranger – had managed
to assert himself in just forty-eight hours. In forty-
eight hours he had made himself at home and
imprinted himself on everything, he delighted some
and entertained others, whereas André-Pierre
himself, who had known the family for more than

ten years, still felt just as uncomfortable, just as out of place, never attuned to what anyone here was thinking or doing, not even his wife, or his own children . . . That was what really sickened him, the ease with which Boris pleased all of them, whether it was with late-night walks or repairing boats, whether it was sunbathing as good as naked or diving headlong into the swimming pool, this guy was the ideal friend . . . and why not lover, or son-in-law.

Taking refuge in the half-light, he now felt more laughable than ever, hopelessly ill-adapted – with or without his tetany, he was already prepared to concede that. This Boris was certainly more at home here than he himself was. The image that kept coming to mind was of a wild animal encroaching on another's territory, one of those big predators whose only objective is to dominate the pack, to round up the females and identify prey . . . Perhaps the girls were watching him at work right now, perhaps they were even on board, with him at the controls, stripped to the waist, holding someone else's 200 horsepower in his hands . . .

'But the boat hasn't been serviced for two years, he's completely crazy, please go and tell him, for God's sake . . .'

The mother was a little disappointed to see André-Pierre so worked up, particularly as he usually showed such restraint; his impassivity and his good manners made up for his being so distant.

She'd accepted he wasn't a demonstrative man but so far he'd always been reliable and reassuring. She would never have suspected that he could be so doleful and disconcerted, so close to tears . . .

She took his hand and asked him what was wrong. With as much compassion as she could muster, she went so far as to ask him to confide in her for once, to let himself go.

'I don't know, of course it's just a feeling, but I think there's something suspect about this Boris. In any event, I'm absolutely sure he never set foot at Buzenval.'

The two sisters hurtled down the stairs, radiant, skipping playfully. They were wearing identical dresses, beach dresses in baby blue, which revealed their tanned legs. Every day they waited till the very end of the afternoon before going down to the beach. André-Pierre said he was surprised they were not taking the children with them and that was when they replied with perfect insouciance, the kind of indolence that takes over after smoking a joint: 'Oh, but they went out in the boat, why . . .'

When, on top of that, he discovered that the father-in-law was not on board, that his two children had therefore been handed over to that madman, that crackpot who was completely out of it, probably doing more than thirty knots roaring over the sea peppered with reefs, that maniac who was more than likely planning to kidnap the children before he got round to doing away with the brother-in-law . . . Suddenly he had the strength to get back up.

Through the bay window you could see the whole of the bay, miles and miles of glinting sea, and on it a myriad little boats heading in every direction, creating an indecipherable game of jackstraws with their wakes. Speedboats plying ahead of their zips of foam, sailing boats gliding gently, others lying at anchor further out, far too many of them probably, and, seen from here, all so small and virtually identical. On top of that the low-lying sun smacked off the water as if it were a mirror, it seemed every fragment of salt had started to twinkle, obscuring the view with their glittering.

He had become so agitated that he had succeeded in sowing doubt in the others' minds, especially as the children had not taken their life jackets. To make them feel even more guilty he implied that, anyway, with what they'd been smoking, they wouldn't have a proper grasp of the situation; to needle them even further he pointed to the wretched things: two pitiful little waistcoats hanging like paltry nets of fish, so empty they seemed pathetic.

Anxiety is the drop of lemon juice that turns the

whole jug of milk, one little premonition and the whole summer can capsize, suddenly the shrieks outside were no longer cheerful but acidic, the sea was too deep, the sun out of place . . . Vanessa was infuriated by her husband's alarmist suggestions and snapped angrily that she was fed up with living with a kill-joy, but at the same time she could not help feeling guilty, guilty also for these skimpy little dresses that they had spent so long choosing, guilty for the half-hour spent trying everything on, thinking about looking attractive, pleasing . . .

Standing at the edge of the gardens they turned a full circle, looking at the entire panorama. Their eyes stinging with the bright reflections, they swept the whole vista looking for the Riva. All they could find to help them see into the distance were the children's pink plastic binoculars, a flimsy little toy which André-Pierre snatched up with savage emotion. The pink binoculars passed from one pair of hands to the other; hopeless, you couldn't see anything through them.

As she cleared away the small first aid kit that she had spread out at the foot of the sofa, the mother thought all this over. She was more worried about André-Pierre than anything else. It was becoming clear to her that he was more vulnerable, more defenceless than she had imagined. This lack of composure, this vulnerability, and the fact that he could be so unsettled by the first stranger who happened to turn up, it all made quite a dent in the image she had of him. Until then she had thought of him as one of the pillars of the family, as well as the company. What she was now discovering about her son-in-law was even more troubling because she expected him to keep an eye on his own wife and children (that went without saying), but also on Philip, and on herself too perhaps . . . As for having doubts about this Boris, about a friend of Philip's, as far as she was concerned it amounted to nothing more or less than having doubts about her own son . . .

All the same, she put down the things she was holding, took her glasses from the sideboard in the sitting room and went back upstairs. The door to the children's room was wide open. On the floor there was a terrible jumble of felt-tip pens that had not been there earlier. The photograph of the choir was still there, in the middle of it all, but covered with scribbling and hideous drawings, rows of beards drawn on to the chins of those perfect little communicants . . . Beards not only on chins, but on cheeks too, and noses, entire faces in fact, so that the net effect was of rows of little bodies topped with monstrous scrawlings covering their faces.

For them it was a first. They had never felt anything like it, never experienced such a thrill of speed . . . What a discovery, feeling the smacking against the hull, and the moment of exhilaration as they flew over each wave, the dull hiss as they dropped back down. The other thing that fascinated them was the way the boat went on and on without touching the water, gliding just above it, like the best skim they had ever seen with them substituted for the pebble.

It was even better, even more exciting, than the fairground rides their father always refused them, at least it was a lot more captivating than what they knew of these merry-go-rounds and attractions. Here, a whole new dimension opened up for them, here each shudder was on a completely different scale; the drumming of the engine sent peculiar vibrations through them with an uncontrollable force that they had never felt before; and the moments when they were truly gliding through the air made them shriek involuntarily, shriek and laugh at the same time, laughing with terror or shrieking with joy, they could no longer tell . . . In any event it was a very far cry from tamely floating around on a lilo, from the afternoons spent lulled by the refrain of rippling waves. The blasting fresh air that stung their ears was indefatigable, a slap that lasted several kilometres, just for a laugh. And over and above everything else was the exultant sensation, the certainty that they were doing something wrong . . .

The elements have a way of acknowledging you (once you have looked them in the eye, once you have outclassed them and shrugged them off): they raise the stakes by providing extreme sensations, a tendency that means that – somewhere beyond fear – a great chasm opens up, an avid desire that catapults you way beyond your original intentions. And fear no longer plays any part in all this, it becomes the catalyst that blows everything up to a larger scale, the tantalizing scent that exacerbates the desire. Boris, of course, had a taste for these sensations, he had an unfailing need to take things further, to push each experience to its limits. Once in his possession, it was as if everything became an agent of his unhealthy dissatisfaction, as if anything that came into his grasp had to suffer for it at some stage, fall prey to his insatiable personality.

Eventually the moment came when it all fell apart for the children, suddenly the excesses enjoyed by this large, roaring beast became too much for two little creatures of their age . . . First their bursts of laughter turned to confusion as they gazed limply over the expeditious sea, then all of a sudden they were crying, there were tears, there were screams and incantations. In disjointed little words they begged for their mother, as if she were always close at hand, a sort of ubiquitous presence, as if all they had to do was call for her and the whole hectic ride would come to a stop.

Boris carried on all the more wildly, aiming his curving trajectory towards the sailing boats, targeting the pleasure boats, passing as close to them as possible, rocking their hulls with his choppy wake, as if to sweep aside all of his childhood memories of beaches, the rancorous times spent watching boats from the shore, while his parents suffered none of their insolence, feeling it was extravagant enough being able to waste a handful of days in the sun . . .

But now it was his turn to escape, he was the one carving a path through the water off the beach, this time he was creating the tiresome foam that annoyed everyone, he was the one people were watching from the shore with a mixture of disapproval and envy, he was there holding the wheel with one hand, never more at ease than in this sort of extravagant performance . . .

He had that in him, the need to ruffle feathers, to come right up close to other people as you would to a candle before blowing it out. It was the same with his past, if he did not blow out the last glowing embers, he knew the burning would come back, and wherever he looked he would be burned.

Further out, he went to goad the peaceful flotilla of pleasure boats anchored off-shore, making them rock violently as he sped past them, proving that a flashy 13-metre ketch was nothing compared to the monster churning in his hands, this speedboat that was ready to do anything if you just dared, if you just had the courage to pull the throttles right out, two little ivory handles, so perfectly smooth and round in your hand, so docile they were insolent . . . In amongst all this the children's screams were just another note of frenzy, drowned out by the others, going completely unnoticed.

The father climbed back up from the boathouse on the narrow flight of steps carved into the rock. When he reached the house there was something about his wife's face that did not suit her, a shadow over those features that had always displayed the view that everything was fine. She glanced at the clothes slung over the father's shoulder (Boris's trousers and shirt), before whipping them into the washing machine. However assiduously she turned out the pockets and delved into the corners, she found nothing, just some traces of tobacco dust, a packet of cigarettes and a packet of roll-up papers.

'It does seem strange, though, that he goes out without a wallet, without any form of identity, and no money on him . . .'

The only reply the father gave was a sigh balanced somewhere between despair and irony. By way of comment, he said that he was feeling absolutely great, better than ever, in fact he was going up to his room to try and lay his hands on the papers for the Riva, after all he might have it serviced so that he could use it again. At least, seeing it out of the boathouse had made him feel like doing something.

Outside, André-Pierre could not stand still for a moment, he kept on peering across the bay, walking from one side to the other to comb through each section of the panorama. Seeing him through the bay window, the mother entertained the idea, an obscure thought, which she quickly shrugged off, but it had come to her all the same, wondering how he would behave in extreme circumstances. How

116

would he react if someone ever threatened his children? How far would he go to get them back . . . ? It was stupid, so stupid that she saw in it the stamp of this ineffectual son-in-law, the surreptitious wrong he was doing them all with his fears and suspicions; that was all his attitude boiled down to in the end – ruining an idyllic afternoon, a perfect part of the holidays, by contaminating everyone with his self-serving doubts . . .

She already hated herself for thinking like that.

Now, for the first time, she hated him.

It was Vanessa who spotted the Riva heading back over from the west, storming straight towards them . . . Seeing this sight through the binoculars, with those two little creatures bouncing about on the rear seats, she uttered an involuntary cry of joy. She handed the binoculars to Julie straight away. As for André-Pierre, he didn't want them. He followed the whole scene listlessly from afar, too weak now to feel any anger or forgiveness. In fact, he was disappointed and annoyed that this meant he was losing not only an excuse for resenting the man but also his unique opportunity to see him loathed by all the others.

It was certain that when the facts were known they would lay the blame on him. He was no longer really sure of anything else, though; not even his own intuitions, nor whether he had actually had any, except for those he had had about this family, the certainty that had crept over him when he very first started working for them, realizing just how God-given the configuration was, that it could provide a frame-work for him to supersede his ambitions. Looking back, he was well aware of how calculated his manoeuvres had been and, if he was honest with himself, he had no illusions about his own character, he knew he was a master of strategy, hence his obsession for seeing the same trait in others. Only a wolf can truly see the hunger in another.

As it neared the coast, the Riva had slowed down, and it now glided over from the west without a single hiccup, steady and level on the smooth water, driven impeccably. Standing very upright on the seats and looking over the windscreen were two little gladiators, two conquerors, with their capes billowing in the wind and their swords pointing towards the house, two beautiful outfits fresh from the shop, so spanking new they sizzled with capricious indulgence.

'There they are,' Julie shouted up to her father, who was following the events from his window just above . . .

'I can see, I can see,' he replied, quite calm, observing from his high vantage point the fruitless turmoil that had shaken the household. Still, he had noticed that Boris had come back to the island showing no respect for the channel, way outside the buoys, which – given that the tide was on the way out – was incredibly irresponsible, it had to be said.

It must have been nearly the tenth time a voice had called to them from the terrace asking them all to sit down for supper, a request that they passed on to one another with a half-hearted sense of urgency, without actually obeying it themselves. As he came out of his room, the father noticed Boris at the other end of the landing, between the double doors into the blue drawing room, which they never used in the summer. Even though he could not see him properly, he could guess with absolute certainty what he was admiring, he knew that he was standing right in front of the display cabinet. Taking small steps, the father walked quietly towards the drawing room, he liked going to some length to produce a surprise . . .

'Aren't you eating then?'

'Oh yes, of course I am. I was just looking.'

'Impressive, aren't they? There's even one from the seventeenth century.'

'Probably that one there?'

'Exactly . . . Do you have any yourself? I mean, do you know something about them?'

'No, not at all.'

'Oh, I could have sworn . . .'

The father slipped his hand behind the glass front and reached for a key with the tips of his fingers.

'Just a precaution, for the children, you see . . . Anyway, the cartridges are in my room, and the bullets too, including the 9mm . . .'

Boris pretended to be interested, especially as the father invited him to shoulder one of the rifles as if he had been a connoisseur.

'Don't you notice anything strange?'

'No.'

'The three barrels: two are smooth and one is rifled . . .'

Boris feigned a nod of admiration.

'And what's that for?'

'It's to have two different calibres – one large and one small – on the same gun. When you're shooting game you never know exactly what you're going to find.'

'Do you shoot?'

'Let's say it's been a family tradition, but I personally have only shot the sort of game that sees me as its prey . . . And there's no shortage of that on my estate, you know, particularly the wild boar, nothing annoys me more than predators like that who destroy everything, completely indiscriminately . . .'

Boris pretended to aim at a piece of china on the far side of the room, and the father kept on adjusting his position as if he really were going to fire at it.

'No, put your hand a bit further along, lower your arm a little, that's it . . .'

'It all comes down to self-defence, then . . .'

'You've got it in one. And you, do you shoot?'

'No.'

'I would have thought . . .'

'I've never been shooting.'

'There must be some game you would be interested in . . .'

'Well . . .'

'No, don't go to such lengths to give me an answer, don't try and come up with something just to please me.'

A voice from the terrace begged them to come to the table. Boris took this opportunity to put the rifle back into the cabinet.

'Just a minute, just shoulder this one with the sights for me, would you? It's very light, isn't it? It's just right for someone my age . . . The only problem is it has a terrible recoil, and with my arthritis it's pretty unforgiving.'

'Do you still use it, then?'

'Predators are pretty few and far between on an island . . .'

Boris aimed at the pieces of china one by one, taking a childish delight in the beam of red light as he shifted it from one target to the next – what fun.

'To be honest, it's a bit of a gimmick. There's actually no point in trying to aim at a wild boar with that red light, unless it's co-operative enough to stand still, which they rarely are, animals like that always know when they're being watched, they never settle for a minute. Here, point the beam at the tureen and then try not to move, it's difficult, isn't it?'

Breathless from climbing up the stairs, André-Pierre arrived in time to see this spectacle, Boris shouldering a rifle and sweeping round the room aiming at everything . . . He told them that the mother was waiting for everyone to sit down, that it was becoming rather urgent, not because the soup might go cold but because the gazpacho was in danger of warming up. Without insisting further, he waited for the father to put the rifle back into the cabinet, close the glass front with scrupulous care and slip the key back in its place.

Part II

*'Give me everything and in
exchange I'll protect you . . .'
'From what?'
'From me.'*

S. J.

In the end he succeeded in dragging them all down to the beach, all of them, as if there were nothing better to do, as if that were an end in itself. What was more, he put forward the idea of the picnic, adding that, if possible, they should try to leave pretty early so as to get a good place, and they should take everything they would need by way of food and drink, as if they really were planning to camp there all day. It was all the easier because they only had to climb down the stairs in the cliff and the sand was right there, directly below the house. The madness on this particular occasion derived from the very humility of the project: eating on the beach, like all these other people who do nothing else all summer long, with no plans beyond spending every day by the sea. When he had touted the idea the previous evening, they had all been surprised but were, in fact, very quickly convinced, realizing that the fact that they had not spent a single day on the beach for all these years was because no one had ever thought to do it.

Watching the preparations, the father felt as if he had gone back in time to the days when he had had to go with the children, when they wanted to swim in the sea, the days before the boats had been bought or the swimming pool built. The girls had dug out the raffia mats, which had not been used for years; they wore simple dresses over their flimsy bikinis, buttoned up the front. André-Pierre no longer dared to intervene. André-Pierre went with the flow. For fear of appearing too obviously dissident he did not offer the least resistance, he had even armed himself with a couple of books, just to pass the time, a novel and a chess manual, which he dived into straight away, finding it hard to understand the facility all the others had for throwing themselves into the water, these people who did not even seem to mind exposing themselves in swimming things, scant clothing that he himself tolerated with difficulty. He could not bear the sun and thought the sea always too cold. The worst thing about it was the near carnival atmosphere that hung over everything . . . all these people in their underwear, and kids everywhere, always screeching and running in every direction, kids splashing each other, spraying each other, flitting from the sand to the sea without even noticing the transition, kids who behaved as if they owned

the place, who even ran over other people's feet —
yes, even that — showering them with sand or
water, in an atmosphere of total permissiveness.
Out of the corner of his eye he watched this family
to which he belonged, watched them with even
more incredulity than he had the day before, no
longer recognizing himself in it at all. It was true
that Boris was perfect in this configuration, setting
a rhythm to the children's games, finding things for
them to do; ever attentive to the father who was
taking an absurdly long time getting into the water;
always finding the right thing to say. He even
teased the mother, quite openly: while she con-
scientiously swam parallel to the shore, he had fun
swimming underneath her and popping up just in
front of her, and it made her laugh. Same thing with
the sisters, and it made them laugh, completely
ridiculous . . .

In this setting, Boris was more animated than
ever, darting from the water to the beach as if there
were no distinction, equally at ease in both, even
managing to light a cigarette with wet hands, and
go back into the water with it. There are creatures
like that, whose bodies are always in their element;
wherever they are they glide, they move smoothly,
without a hiccup. It was then that, quite paradox-
ically, a feeling of covetousness compounded his
disgust. There was no denying that seeing him
like that — with the honeyed tan of his shoulders,

the moulded outline of his muscles, the harmony emanating from every pose he assumed – he could understand why a woman might want to touch.

Between men, this sort of fascination can engender a desire to spend time with another man, to become mates, to have a share in another man's strengths just by being near him. In fact, that sort of man is never short of muckers, wherever they go they make friends, they have a sort of natural predisposition to it, a peculiar attractiveness. Being seen with this looker meant you could appropriate some of his power, share in his prominence. There was no question that Philip, who was so easily influenced, had felt this attraction; Philip who was always on the look out for anything that glittered, who revered power (whatever form it took), and valued anything that might in any way show him in a favourable light.

The two sisters were playing in the waves with the children, the father was taking his rheumatism for a stroll along the shoreline, Boris was chatting with the mother under the parasol near by, he was telling her about shiatsu, offering to relax her by running his palms over particular parts of her body, between the shoulder blades, he pointed to the area he meant . . . The guy had an unbearable mania for touching, this way of seeing everything as accessible. André-Pierre found it more and more difficult to concentrate on his chess problem, feeling uncomfortable so close to the mother-in-law and this man who now really was massaging her, exploring her back with his hands, allegedly to relax her. In any event the mother had closed her eyes, genuinely relaxed.

André-Pierre shrugged dismissively. He lay down and put his book over his eyes. Soothed by the constant refrain of the waves and the gentle breath of wind, he tried to expel all resentment. He knew everything that was going on from the sounds: the father talking to goodness knows who, the twins whining, the sisters chatting quietly, the mother laughing occasionally. For the first time he actually let himself go, started falling asleep, on a beach, in the middle of all those people—

'So, you little bugger, taking it easy, are you?'

Hearing these words he sat bolt upright.

No. Boris was still crouching next to the mother, kneading the nape of her neck.

The voice must have come from somewhere else, from those people next door, or them over there.

Once dinner was over, while everyone was still languishing at the table, lulled to a greater or lesser extent by the balmy night air, André-Pierre was up on the first floor restoring the photograph with solvent. He had always had a weakness for games that required precision, model aircraft in his childhood, chess problems, then he had pursued his studies with the same application, and the whole rest of his life had gone on from there.

The meticulous care he had taken was beginning to pay off. The red and yellow beards gradually wore away under the cotton wool, disappearing one by one. Under one green beard he even recognized Philip, more than fifteen years on. When it came down to it, he had not actually changed that much, still the same nonchalance, the same insolence in refusing to pose. Following on from this familiar face were rows of other faces, each as prepubescent as the last, each as inoffensive and utterly unknown to him, but in all those faces there was not one hint of this other man, even in the last row. And yet life would have been so much more simple if he had been there, if there could have been the tiniest correspondence with what he claimed.

However hard he tried to shave them all and to restore the photograph as best he could, once the choir was completely revealed, one thing at least was clear: in amongst all those faces there was one that did not feature, unless you could accept that he had changed a great deal, unless you could really persuade yourself of that.

That was when everything turned upside down once again, suppositions swept back over him like a headache, because, if this guy had never been to Buzenval, if they hadn't met there, then it was strange that he wasn't worried about Philip's imminent arrival. Although you couldn't exactly say he was waiting for him, he didn't seem to be apprehensive about him either . . . Or perhaps they were in it together, they had agreed everything, honed this whole manoeuvre to target him, André-Pierre.

Someone downstairs was calling him to come and have coffee, but rather than going down he ran himself a bath, so that he could mull over his theories. The sounds from the table came in through the window. Once again the girls couldn't stop laughing, in that exaggerated way, no question he'd got them smoking again, they must have rolled themselves a joint on the quiet, sneakily beside the pool, he'd caught them huddled together there a few times, enveloping each other in their wreaths of exhaled smoke.

Once he had sunk into the bubbles, too tense to let himself relax fully, he felt more isolated than ever, peaceful in himself, but so naked it made him shiver . . . He ran a little more hot water. In the snatches of conversation he suddenly realized that he could no longer pick out Boris's voice; the girls, the father, the mother and the two children, yes, but not the other man. It was a few minutes now since he had heard him, not the briefest burst of laughter, nor a snatch of his voice, unless he had left the table, or was in the house perhaps, just outside the . . . He was probably just being silly but, all the same, André-Pierre climbed out of the bath to bolt the door more securely. What was really eating at him was the fact that he couldn't say anything, he couldn't reveal everything he knew about Philip and his errant ways. When all was said and done, no one knew anything about his scams, no one suspected just how much he, André-Pierre, had to do to keep Philip away, paying him off, even paying the lawyer, without whom he would have gone down

134

not for ten months but two years . . . The father, who did keep an eye on the movement of capital, thought that all those regular payments to an interest account with the American Bank were only there in preparation for possible acquisitions in the New World, some money in the vanguard so to speak . . . He had never talked to him about money paid directly to Philip . . . In fact, so long as Philip stayed away, so long as he bloody well left him in peace to get on with business matters, André-Pierre would keep all these stories to himself: a perfectly watertight operation.

As the water cooled, he found it difficult to imagine what Philip would gain by sending a henchman . . . To get more money? To frighten him? And if the heavy was waiting for an opportunity to show his hand, then why didn't he take the initiative? Unless he was deliberately taking his time, enjoying all the comforts, appropriating them to some extent, taking advantage of the pool, the boat, the surroundings, and why not everything else . . . ?

That made him sit up with a start in the bath, so that he could listen more clearly, at least, because he was no longer really sure that he could hear Vanessa's voice either. It's true, it was a good few minutes now since he had heard her. As he realized this he gave a sort of shudder, a little spasm that ran down his back. Probably the tetany . . . He closed the window.

With the water becoming cooler around him, he gave a free rein to his disturbing intuitions and realized that it would not be long before there was some concrete fact for him to hold on to, somehow or other he would have to confront the situation, whatever it might be, to prepare himself for the worst, why not? He who had always thought of these holidays as the ultimate seclusion, who with-drew every year into this cosy configuration where nothing threatened him, at a safe distance from the Greek gods on the beaches and the people touting for trade; holidays that actually served as a metaphor for his life, and now for once he was afraid . . . Having this Boris here was worse than an intruder, a cockroach between silk sheets . . .

He thought he heard two people speaking to each other on the landing, footsteps absorbed by the carpeting . . . And so what?

Looking at the facts head-on would change nothing. This guy had managed to integrate himself; now that that was a given, he would just have to cope with it, to wait for the hate to be kindled, and to leave it to spread.

He would have liked some sort of consolation for his lack of courage, to fly into a filthy rage, to tell this Boris that he just didn't like him, to ask him to clear off, to talk to him man to man. Quite simple sentences when it came down to it, but so hard to say.

Not to mention that very soon Philip would have to be included in the equation, and this time Philip would probably be ten times the man with his ally on board. With two of them against one it would be even more unfairly weighted . . .

The water was freezing now, he was shivering; unable to control himself, he shuddered . . . Unless Philip wasn't coming.

When you go for a walk at the very end of the evening – embracing the darkened countryside with slow, careful footsteps – you can step outside and beyond things: time no longer matters, you fall into profane meditation while everything sleeps and you sink into that tiredness.

That evening the father did not feel like walking. All he wanted to do was to stay there, enjoying the coolness coming up from the lawn, listening out for the halting murmur of the sea, which was quite motionless that evening. As for the mother, she never went for evening walks. Perhaps because she was afraid of the dark, but mostly because she was anxious to help the housekeeper in the kitchen so that she did not have to stay too late.

That evening Julie had also decided to stay at home; not even claiming to be tired, she just wanted to chat with her father . . . But Vanessa and Boris had set off on the side of the cliff over there, along the little path that hugged the shoreline.

In that direction the coast was completely open and deserted, not a single house to interrupt the vast horizon of the sea, and no true beach either, squeezed between the rocks and the ocean.

Boris did not know this particular spot. What he did know, though, was that there are times when the question of scruples is allayed by the magic of the moment, a distance you can suddenly establish from yourself, a circumstantial sense of permissiveness. As if the simple fact of brushing close to an unfamiliar body somehow divorces you from your own remorse, your own virtue. Vanessa had been well aware of how close he and her sister had come the other evening, she had heard quite clearly the toing and froing on the landing, which had been far from discreet. She knew she was straying on to a path that had already been explored, the only risk she was running was that she might get caught up in the game. At her feet, the tiny creases of waves rippled inconsequentially.

Vanessa fully realized that if she took this man's arm Julie would know about it, perhaps she could already tell. That evening she wanted to feel the same desire, to share in the same sensations – then, at least, they would be all the more complicit: complicit in this skin, complicit in arriving at the same point, confronting the same danger, against the same chest, because that was where her head now lay, against this man's chest, where hers had not been yesterday, but another's had, caught in the contours of the same spell.

And there was the sea: she had dreamed of seeing it like this for so long, seeing it under the effects of this particular position, with her head on a man's knee and that distraction in her eyes, acknowledging a whole world before her that she could never embrace but knowing that what lay close beside her was infinitely more disturbing.

She had pictured her sin differently . . . Having imagined it a thousand times, she had seen herself throwing herself at a man who was beautiful, yes, but above all unbridled, avid, violent even; and abandoning herself to him in the demented fulfilment of a shared longing . . . Whereas now she was not even moving. Neither was he. He was only just stroking her hair, although he did so with undeniable application, a sign that this man had a sense of the value of things, he was not the sort of man to abuse a situation, to cheapen these moments, adrift, with banal behaviour . . . Quite the opposite, this man understood all the significance of the moment, as if gauging how exclusive this form of abandon was, as if he knew that this was a first for her . . . His restraint moved her more than anything else, empathy compounded her desire, persuading her not to hold back . . . Then a hand touched her insistently for the first time, a hand remoulded her body without missing any part of her – particularly as this hand was powerful, a hand designed to be courageous, a demanding hand that did not force her but nevertheless imposed itself on her, irresistibly, a hand instantly familiar, a hand that made her give up any idea of reticence, two hands now . . . All at once he had trodden that slender path between ambush and bewitching, between domination and abandonment . . . Little by little she felt herself succumbing, the longing to give in came to her as naturally as an impatient outburst, a crescendo of positions that could no longer bear to wait . . . Suddenly she wanted him, suddenly she hungered for this body, this body she clung to to avoid suffering the rugged surface of the rock beneath her. Then she wanted the rock too, she wanted to be pinned between these two rocks, the one rigid and cold, the other as supple as it was breathless, a rock with its man's tentacles coiled round her and bearing her into the sea; she was now leaning against the water, disorientated as all her points of reference dissolved, bathing in complete abandon, no longer wanting anything but this, deeply inhaling the evening air as she drowned a little, taking the water from his mouth and then breathing at last, coming back without screaming in panic, catching her breath under the surface, suffocating, floating for a while in the transition between life and asphyxia, and letting herself be taken, unable to gain any purchase on the surface, drowning in something that was no longer water . . . Even this did not make her afraid of these arms, these arms which held the power of life and death, but which brought her back at the last moment, these arms in which she was helpless . . . She glided like that for a long time, between his skin and the sea, abandoned by all certainty, but thrilled by everything else, especially discovering she could breathe again. This man was the summer itself, whether naked or clothed, with his tanned skin and his salty smile, his hair that was too short to offer any hold other than the nape of his neck, and driving himself further and further into her. The time came when she realized she was no longer in her depth, she no longer had the least purchase on any element at all, except for him: his power of life and death was now complete, it didn't matter to her.

Julie was all alone now. Sitting in the dancing light of the torches, she did not even feel sorry for herself. She was doing nothing, just waiting for them. She would probably see them coming back over there. At first the light would be too bright for them, and they would rub their eyes. Then they would grow accustomed to it as each footstep brought them closer. They would each have dropped the other's hand that they held. They wouldn't even try to piece together a facial expression, some way of hiding things, anything. They would sit down here, perhaps not even side by side, wouldn't speak straight away, and would both have the same faded smile, the same hint of embarrassment fading from their non-committal faces. They would look beautiful. They would be thirsty. They wouldn't be long now.

She didn't feel like sleeping alone tonight.

'Boris who?'

He did not know.

'And how long has he been missing?'

'He isn't missing, you see he's up at the house.'

'All right then. So, you want us to make enquiries about some man whose name you don't know but who's staying in your house . . .'

'But I'm Monsieur Chassagne's son-in-law, I mean . . .'

'I know, I know, but that's not a good enough reason for us to make enquiries about all and sundry. If you could lodge some sort of complaint, then fine, but failing that . . . We're not an information service.'

'But couldn't you possibly question him, just like that, find out what he's doing here? Ask him for his papers, I don't know . . .'

'Listen, I'll say it again, and despite the respect I feel for your family, I can't do anything for you, and

144

when it comes to knowing the names of people in your house and finding out why they're there, I'm going to make a very simple suggestion: you'll just have to ask them yourself.'

The policeman said this with just enough irony to regret it instantly.

'You know we've always been very understanding with you, last year we didn't even notify anyone about your brother-in-law when, to be quite frank, people shouldn't go setting off fireworks when they're half drunk, and without any authorization to boot. No, honestly, I can assure you that we're always happy to help you, but frankly, there's a difference between that and asking for papers from someone who's staying with you . . . And, anyway, what have you got against this man?'

André-Pierre gave no reply, in all likelihood feeling too offended. Mainly because he couldn't see, he just couldn't see how to formulate all his suspicions without appearing over the top, fanciful or paranoid. When all was said and done, there wasn't really anything he could hold against the man, no proof beyond the fact that he couldn't find him on a photograph; the only things he could reproach him for were the way he cheated at tennis and his aptitude for wandering about the place stripped to the waist, that ostentatious manner that was so extraordinarily natural, so casual that it was disgusting . . . Or he could mention the way he buzzed around Julie, and his wife, too, but to tip over into jealousy here in front of them, that would be obscene . . .

'Mmm? So what's he done to you, then?'

André-Pierre came back out of the police station with his chin tucked into his collar, as if afraid that he might be seen. He knew that this move had achieved nothing, that he could rely only on himself to back up his suspicions, to accumulate proof, and – depending on how that went – to act, and to stop avoiding the situation.

Inside, the two policeman were already discussing it as if it were a joke. The sergeant who had been over to the Chassagnes' was convinced that it was all to do with bedroom-hopping; with people like them, everything boiled down to that in the end, you'd think they had nothing better to do with their time.

His colleague would have willingly shared his view, and yet he had sensed the fear weighing down on André-Pierre, a hidden fear, like you sometimes get with people who come to lodge a complaint but who retract it at the last moment, suddenly realizing the significance of what they are doing, people who panic when they hear the word statement, the minute they see the formal semantics, the punctilious vocabulary used to qualify crimes and offences.

'With some of them, just the word's enough to frighten them off.'

When he arrived back, André-Pierre found an effervescence, a general feverishness, hanging over everything. Thanks to this atmosphere, he understood before anyone even told him. Every family harbours its animosities, every community ferments its antagonisms, but the moment one of their number comes to join them for a holiday, the minute they meet with someone after a long separation, the enthusiasm of the moment outweighs the reasons they have for resenting them; that is how we find ourselves trapped within the mirage created by reunions.

Boris came down the stairs striking an imperial figure on the staircase, still buttoning up his shirt (which André-Pierre recognized as one of the Dior shirts Vanessa had given him, the white one with discreet finishing). Boris affected an air of complete relaxation, an apparent self-satisfaction, troubled by nothing, as if he were at home. When he saw that André-Pierre was back from Paimpol, he favoured him with an excessively friendly thump on the back.

'So, good walk?'

André-Pierre felt the full weight of the hidden meaning, but he couldn't guess where it came from, how could he? Feeling as uncomfortable as an unwanted guest, he didn't know where to go or what to do, an outsider in the ambient feverishness, unable to integrate himself in it.

'A little Martini, how does that sound?'

He just shrugged his shoulders.

'Suit yourself, I'm pouring myself one.'

The two sisters were tidying the sitting room, busying themselves as if for some great occasion, having done themselves up beautifully once again, yet another provocation.

Trying not to clash too obviously with the general mood, he asked what time Philip was coming. The mother did not know the exact time, but what was quite certain was that he had just rung the ironmonger to check that all the rockets had been delivered all right.

'In fact, he also asked whether you could go over and pick them up. Since the boat's working again, you could possibly go with Boris. I hope you wouldn't mind too much.'

He tried to find some excuse to decline, but the mother was already patting his cheek gratefully.

He really took some persuading. You would have thought he was afraid of the boat now, or was suddenly worried about being sea-sick. The problem was that Boris had already taken the controls, but André-Pierre was determined to drive, especially as he knew the Riva by heart, having handled it frequently back in the days when he was still wooing his wife, a time when he would not have hesitated to spend a whole afternoon looking for the most inaccessible creek. That was in the days when he did not even think about wearing life jackets, the days when – even though he had no idea of how to talk to women – he did at least know how to put them in unusual settings, which would give him an advantage. The effort he used to put into preparing the scene . . . In those days he was the one who took the initiative, Vanessa just followed him, not afraid of being bored, overjoyed in fact (or very nearly) because even if she did know in advance that this man would never really make her happy, she at least felt balanced, content . . . At the time, that in itself was quite something.

In the end it was the children who forced him to go, the children who couldn't understand why Daddy was refusing to pick up all the lovely red and blue rockets to light up the sky tomorrow night, why would he deny them that pleasure . . . ?

Boris kept revving the accelerator as he waited coolly for the other man to make up his mind, not actually intervening, forcing himself to smile – albeit ironically. Once André-Pierre had resolved to climb aboard, Boris hardly gave him time to lift his second leg over the side before pulling the throttle right out. André-Pierre was hurled on to the rear seat and he begged Boris to stop and turn back, terrified by the realization that he had left his life jacket behind.

Wedged awkwardly on his back, he watched through the spray of water churned out by the boat as his children grew smaller, his children who were waving goodbye to him, his children who appeared blurred and diffuse through this fountain spurting up to the sky. Boris deliberately took each wave head on, whooping like a cowboy with every rodeo buck.

Once again André-Pierre saw the measure of the man's recklessness, and yet again he was paying the price for it; it was enough to make him think the lunatic had descended on him like a curse, one of those evils that targets you one day and then never lets go; it was enough to make him think the guy was only there to persecute him, or to fulfil some malicious intent. He stared at Boris, perfectly incredulous, unable to take his eyes off him, feeling as if he were living a sequence in a film that had nothing to do with him. André-Pierre lay across the seat, holding on to it as best he could while the other man took his perversion so far that he wasn't even sitting on the seat but right on the edge, virtually out of the boat, as if wanting to be buffeted and whipped by as much of the stream of air as possible, doubling the thrill . . . Boris was talking to him, but without turning to look at him. André-Pierre could not hear a word of what he was saying, but he was still quite sure that he was taunting him once again, he would be referring to him as Gramps – or worse – there was no doubt about it. Boris thought he was a pathetic joke and kept on belittling him by calling him AP . . .

André-Pierre got up to come to the front of the boat, and just as he was climbing over the front seat a violent impact threw him into the air; he barely had to exaggerate his trajectory in order to come crashing into Boris, who hurtled straight into the drink, with an inanimate thud, already far behind in the wake . . .

There is nothing worse that those involuntary gestures that betray everything you are really thinking. For a couple of seconds he thought he might just carry on. For a couple of seconds he thought he might speed off as if nothing had happened, but he couldn't possibly take responsibility for this, especially as he hadn't done it on purpose; it wasn't even as if he had really taken his revenge or had a rush of blood to the head, he had just lost his balance . . .

He eased off the throttle and made a sharp U-turn. Boris was still very much there, unsinkable, unshakeable, not at all deflated by fear or disbelief; in fact he was amusing himself spitting great fountains of water, happy as a toddler in the bath. André-Pierre approached him slowly, with the same feeling of disgust he would have going back to check on an animal he had knocked down on the road. Not knowing what would be the right thing to say in the situation, he affected the half-concerned, half-astonished expression of someone who cannot believe what has happened. He even went so far as to apologize: he said he was sorry for being so clumsy.

Once he was close to Boris he cut the engine and steadied the boat as best he could to hold out his hand to him. The other man took hold of him with a fierce grip.

'So, Gramps, what got into you . . . ?'

He hardly had time to feel the mixture of anger and disgust bubbling up again before he was flying overboard, launched by the monstrous strength in the other man's arm, realizing suddenly just how cold the water was.

Lulled by the hubbub on the beach – a noisy combination of children's games and rolling waves – both girls were looking forward to seeing their brother again. They wondered what sort of behaviour Philip would have in store for them this year. Would he serve up his relatively unsubtle hippy pose, not even trying to disguise the fact that he keeps overfilling his glass, and rolling his joints at the table, the outdated minor excesses of a make-believe rebellion, dissipations that don't actually shock anyone any longer? Or would he be the spoilt child trying terribly hard to be good: the gentle obedient son who manoeuvres to get what he wants . . . another year of financial support?

Unless he turns out to be completely uncontrollable yet again, in which case they would have to hide the key to the bar and stay up to all hours of the night worrying that he hadn't come home. Or perhaps they should leave the key, let him drink there on the spot, then at least they could sleep in peace, knowing he was in the house . . .

The ironmonger was not amused when they turned up soaked from head to foot, right in the middle of his break as well. And he must have told them a thousand times he wouldn't be open until four o'clock, that he didn't want to be disturbed before then under any circumstances. Mind you, coming from that family, nothing surprised him any more. And, anyway, he'd had enough of doing them this favour; in fact, just like every year, he assured them that this would be the last time, that next year they would just have to order their explosives for themselves. André-Pierre, standing dripping in his shirt and trousers (having not had the courage to turn up in boxer shorts like Boris), was so embarrassed that he suggested they came back later. Boris, on the other hand, was already inside, wandering round the shop, inspecting the place, much to the owner's indignation – you would have thought the man hadn't heard a thing he'd said. He walked all round the shop, touching everything, hypnotized by the abundance of curiosities in it, fascinated by the assortment of tools, like a child in a toy shop. Chains, cables, screw-drivers, hammers, crowbars, all those gleaming surfaces in chrome and steel, everything shining, made precious by its new-ness . . . He weighed up the tools one by one,

155

appreciating them as precision instruments, trying to identify the one that suited him best in his hand. A new hammer is a beautiful thing. Hammers are usually slightly worn, crooked or working loose on the handle, but this one was utterly immaculate, the steel pure with absolutely no rust, the handle impeccable, all varnished wood, as smooth and blunt as the body of a spanking new wife . . . He also picked up a number of crowbars of varying sizes, in cold metal; just holding a thing like that produces a kind of energy, a resolve that almost drives you to use it, to use it on anything that comes to hand, even if it is only breaking open the nailed lids of the cases of rockets.

Boris put the largest one on the counter, and – as if stating the obvious – told André-Pierre to include it on the bill, not even mentioning reimbursement. Out of bravado, André-Pierre refused, even if only to establish some authority in front of the shopkeeper.

'And how, pray, are we going to open the cases tomorrow night?'

'All right then, add it on.'

In order to have done with them as quickly as possible, the ironmonger decided to bring the cases out himself. He called from the back of the shop, asking them to help him. Boris curtly snatched the heavy boxes from him.

'Don't go hurting yourself . . .'

He carried the cases two by two to the quay opposite, and piled them haphazardly on the boat in the full glare of the sun. Meanwhile, André-Pierre just couldn't lay his hands on his wallet and his credit card holder. When he realized they were gone, he very soon started cursing Boris, tempted by easy accusations, flashing a nasty look at him as he came back over to the shop . . . But it can't have been that, actually, he must have lost them earlier, when they went for their little dip, ditto his mobile, which he couldn't find, the whole lot must be lying five metres down . . .

The longer he ruminated on it, the more securely the certainty anchored itself: there are some people in life who just don't suit you, it can't be helped, they're quite simply ill-fated creatures and you compromise yourself just by coming into contact with them, every second spent with them brings you closer to danger.

'Don't worry about it . . . We'll stop on the way back . . .'

'For goodness sake, that doesn't make any sense, we'd never find the spot . . .'

'Well, I would. Only about ten metres from the buoy by the *Lady's Thigh*, the fifth one along the channel. Don't fuss about it, a good mask and we can dive for them. By the way, would you have that, a mask and a snorkel?'

*   *   *

157

Only his chequebook was still safely there in his back pocket. André-Pierre flicked through it to find the driest cheque, the most presentable one.

'Should I include the mask and the snorkel?'

Boris confirmed that there was no point gift-wrapping them, they were to be used straight away. As he passed him, he tried to slip the snorkel over André-Pierre's head, André-Pierre who – for once – would have no part in his prank, surprising himself with the vehemence of his evasive shrug, scuffling in a way he probably had not done since he was a boy . . .

Seeing the pen fail to make any mark on the sodden paper was the last straw for the shopkeeper. As if it would somehow mollify him, André-Pierre launched into a conversation: in a voice that was intended to be casual he asked when Philip had called. The ironmonger, busy wafting the cheque in the air, replied that he had first called two days ago, and then again this morning, to make sure everything was good and ready . . .

'And where would you say he was calling from?'

'Well, from here, in God's name . . .'

'He rang you from Paimpol?'

'Rang? No, no, he called in.'

On the other side of the shop window, Boris stood with two cases in his arms, challenging passing cars with his usual swagger, pretending to kick out at those that did not stop, animating the quiet street with this parody of a row, probably just to show himself off to the tourists watching from the café terrace, particularly two girls he had spotted.

'And the crowbar, I imagine you won't be taking that . . . It doesn't matter, I'll put it back where it belongs.'

'No, actually, I will take it.'

'As you like.'

Once it was all loaded up, once the cases were all more or less securely stacked on the rear seat (cruelly compromising the boat's draught), Boris decided to go and have a drink at that particular terrace along the port. André-Pierre retorted that it was unthinkable to leave such an arsenal out in the sun, and anyway he couldn't stand wandering round in his wet clothes any longer, dripping in every direction and feeling disheveled. Boris watched him complaining yet again, with more irony than compassion; almost with disgust, in fact, probably enjoying provoking him all the more. As far as he was concerned, he had decided to have a drink, and nothing would stop him from doing just that. André-Pierre might well have been whingeing, he might well have been trying to make Boris feel sorry for him by wringing the water out of his sleeves, that did not alter the fact that, once again, he seemed to be trotting along behind him. This made André-Pierre loathe the intruder even more, resenting more than ever his regal detachment, his manifest lack of concern . . . And yet – without any kind of order or injunction – there he was following him.

He led him over to a table where three young tourists – two girls and a boy – were sitting. The boy had his face buried in a guide book, studying the contours of the region. The girls sat back watching people, quite taken by what they perceived as their exoticism, and not even intimidated by this man walking over to them (but rather amused by his acolyte hurrying along behind), set jittering from head to toe by this exciting stranger, by the nerve of any man who took the risk of approaching.

Earlier, they had missed nothing of his coming and going between the shop and boat, or his matador antics with the cars. As well as feeling somewhat perplexed, the boy with the guide book was treated to another source of annoyance: he had to move up a little to make room for Boris. All smiles, Boris sat himself down between the two girls, and guessed – with questionable acuity – that they were American, which was enough to make them laugh. Obscene, thought André-Pierre.

In very hesitant French, they asked Boris whether the boat was his. Not only did he say that it was, he also suggested in a lordly way that he could take them for a spin later. André-Pierre could hardly believe it.

'Come on, you can't just stand there like that, come and sit down with us . . .'

With the enthusiasm of a bearer of great news, Boris told them that he knew the United States well, in fact he had been there only recently, which suddenly introduced a climate of collusion. He smothered both girls with a beaming smile, gave a quick wink to the man, and asked them all what they would like to drink.

The young man asked what all the cases were for.

'Bombs to flush out the terrorist!' Boris replied, boring right into him with his smile, so much so that this boy with the mop of blond hair almost began to feel guilty, he flushed . . . but he did still feel constrained to laugh, and was in fact satisfied to have got a reply. André-Pierre secretly watched the poor man's static defeat, and recognized something of himself in it. In some ways he already felt solidarity for him.

'So, what can we get you to drink?'

They turned to each other to discuss what they were going to drink. Boris flashed a look at André-Pierre to sound out the question of cash, and, without even waiting for a reply, he cut straight through the general confusion with a decisive: 'Champagne!'

*　　*　　*

Having spent so much time watching him, and having been subjected to the full force of his influence, André-Pierre was now reaching a definitive conclusion about this Boris. For the first time he could see that, compared to this man, Philip just didn't make the grade. He couldn't imagine his brother-in-law standing up to him for a moment, couldn't see him resisting at all . . . Next to Boris, Philip must have seemed more like a little kid than ever, more insubstantial, easier to influence; and he very probably had been influenced. There was no question about it, Boris would always play that trick on him too, getting him to pay . . . He was now sure that Boris must have done whatever he wanted with him, more so with him than with anyone else. There are a thousand ways of gaining the upper hand over someone who's a bit of a drifter like Philip, without counting the real drifters who want nothing more than to be dominated.

A guy who can captivate the first girl he bumps into, a guy who can get the ironmonger to open before four o'clock, who can get everyone in this family to like him and be unanimously adopted, and to manage all that in barely two days; he was quite sure that this particular guy did whatever he wanted with other people.

*　　*　　*

For the first time André-Pierre felt compassion for his brother-in-law. Imagining Philip in this bastard's clutches made him feel closer to him, it gave him the touching but inadmissible idea that they were linked, that they were as vulnerable as each other and viewed with the same contempt. Feeling an intimate disgust at this idea, he stood up briskly, clearly implying that he was leaving, and – trying to sound abrupt – he told Boris that he was going home, that he didn't want a drink and that he was fed up with being there . . . Boris's only reply was to give him a sardonic smile while he dangled the keys to the Riva. Then, murmuring it as an order, he told him to sit back down and – more particularly – not to get in the way of the waiter who was just coming up behind him, the man already had enough to cope with, with all those champagne glasses on his tray and the swaying bottle . . .

Being gradually, slowly, dispossessed of every- thing, inexorably overtaken by the situation, and having no other choice than to give in . . . Once again all those images came back to him, the awful memories of school changing rooms when, as a boy, he had been forced to wear those stupid shorts and to run around after a ball . . . And the hearty camaraderie of the whole thing, the atmosphere as leaden as a bad joke, the arrogant way they all seemed so delighted at the mere thought of trampling about on a pitch . . . The only solution he had found had been to injure himself as quickly as possible so that he could go back to the changing rooms. Then he would change back into his clothes and sit there on the bench waiting for them, not even moving, painfully aware that when they came in he would be filled with shame and shyness, knowing that – once again – he would appear ridiculous, ridiculous for being the only one who was dressed in the middle of all these naked, sweating boys (who even went so far as to compare themselves in the showers – and he loathed them for that). He had always promised himself he would have his revenge one day on these boys with their blatant brandishment of their bodies . . .

'Come on then, Gramps, are you going to wake up?'

André-Pierre was startled by a general burst of laughter, and looked around a little wildly. In fact, the *patron* was calling him from the bar, desperately trying to hand him the telephone. A phone call. It was for him. It was from the hotel opposite.

'Hello . . .'

'Philip?'

The girls were both on lilos, drifting to and fro on the pool, letting themselves float from one side to the other, without any effort on their part, just giving a little push with a foot at each edge. Meanwhile the children were playing on the steps into the pool, safe in their rubber rings, occasionally springing up in front of one of the two women. The sun was sinking, drawing out the shadows until they lay full length along the ground, it was that lingering time of day. That was exactly why they had stripped so completely, unashamedly, for the cosmetic pleasure of perfecting their tans, to give some meaning to the boredom. From time to time a breath of wind thwarted their trajectories, pushing them towards the edge or moving them back into the middle of the pool, a sort of game, pure distraction.

At that time of day the sounds coming up from the beach became quieter and quieter. There were no more shrieks of laughter or defiant games in the waves, but softly spoken words scattered about the sand, plans for the evening. Mothers putting things away while their children dressed, munching on biscuits; indolent waves petering out on the beach; and a few dreamy figures who loved the peaceful feeling of being the last in the water, they were usually the quiet sort.

There were no longer any boats out on the water either. No more constant criss-crossing wakes, no more motors whining maddeningly like mosquitoes . . . At this time in the evening, most of the boats had been drawn high up on to the sand, or were at anchor in the middle of the bay, all pointing in the same direction. The hot emerald of the pine trees against the pink granite, the twinkling silica like a shower of sunlight; in all this there was only one wave, one sound, coming from the Riva, which was just peeping into the furthest corner of the scenery, appearing from behind the barrier of the reef, a sound that was all the more throaty because of the weight of the cargo.

The children understood straight away from their mother's reaction . . .

'There they are! There they are!'

Vanessa walked barefoot right to the edge of the lawn. They could see the mahogany hull approaching in the distance, varnished by the sun, gliding without the tiniest shudder. There were two people on board: Philip, who was standing up at the front, and the driver, silhouetted behind the windscreen. With a rush of happiness, Vanessa clearly recognized Philip, and Julie came over to see too, waving her arms expansively. Both of them followed the distant roar of the V8 engine, revving more slowly for once, which gave it a degree of solemnity.

To celebrate, dinner was served on the best table-cloth. They used a few chandeliers as well as the silver, and put the lights on in the bottom of the swimming pool, just to mark the occasion. For once André-Pierre and Philip had spontaneously sat down next to each other. The mother was happy to see this change of attitude in the two men she liked to think of as her 'sons', she saw it as a result of the efforts she had made with André-Pierre; they were undeniably closer. She had wanted to see them like this for such a long time, perhaps not friends, but at least reconciled; complicit in some way. Especially as this evening they did seem to have one thing in common; they both seemed to find it difficult being there, there was an absence in them, a weariness in their expressions . . .

'It's just they weighed a ton, those things . . .' Philip said again, as an excuse.

And it is hard work unloading the cases from the boat on to the pontoon, and then dragging them up

the little creek, getting them up on to the rocks . . .
they really were spent.

The father, the mother, all of them said what a
pity it was that Boris wasn't there, such a nice
meal.

Philip had noticed how disappointed his sisters
looked when he told them that Boris was not
coming back, that he had decided to stay on the
mainland, and that he clearly had not been planning on twiddling his thumbs while he was there
. . . He had also spotted a fair degree of anguish in
his father. The father who was usually so far
removed from everything, the father who spent so
much time in quiet contemplation in his own off-
hand way, and here he was apparently sincerely
distressed that one of his friends wasn't there . . .

'But, he can't be going to spend the night over
there, he didn't even take his things . . . I even seem
to remember he left without a shirt on.'

Everyone agreed, certain they had seen him
leave this afternoon with no shirt or T-shirt, not a
stitch on his back.

'He really can't wander about in his swimming
shorts all night, can he?'

Without much conviction, André-Pierre and
Philip said that he would come back that night, or
a bit later, he wouldn't be long . . . Anyway, the guy
had such a way of sorting himself out that he was
perfectly capable of finding an entire wardrobe,

even without a penny on him, and when the shops were shut.

It was hard not to show anything, stifling the nausea that reared up from time to time, the shell-shocked feeling like after an accident. Philip had often felt it in the early days of his incarceration, the incredulity that grips you, the feeling that it can't be true, an inability to accept your circumstances, to be lucid about your own situation . . .

'Well, I do hope you didn't show him the *Lady's Thigh* . . . The boy's got so much nerve I wouldn't put it past him to try and get home along it . . . It might be wiser to go and fetch him, don't you think?'

'Don't worry about him, Dad, he's not in any danger . . . Anyway, he's a very good swimmer.'

'Even so, it'll be a very high tide tonight . . . and you never know, I mean, if he's had a bit to drink . . .'

The evening dawdled along gently in this way, set to the rhythm of the flickering torches and the chirping crickets. Philip dived headfirst into the pool, saying he was still tired from the journey, still a bit on edge. It was so hot that André-Pierre did the same.

After swimming a couple of lengths, they both turned over and floated on their backs, perfectly synchronized; it was only just possible to hear the quiet sound of the water, the sort of gentle slapping noises you might expect in a bath. The sisters were still sitting at the table, no longer really talking, taking turns to drag on a little joint that they handed to each other discreetly, as they watched those two very familiar bodies floating.

The tide, an especially low tide in fact, had been out for a long time now, and the sea was already beginning to rise, flowing urgently as it usually did in the first couple of hours. The speed of the tide could be assessed from the currents, which smoothed the surface in certain places, flowing against the grain and flattening out like sheet metal, creating channels where the water seemed more dense, and glossy as a piano, a lacquer that betrayed no indication of the danger.

The sea would rise back up like this for six hours, flooding everything and depositing sludge in its depths, filling in the various gulleys and traces of footsteps, erasing the memory of every walk, relentlessly undoing one landscape to super-impose another. And, once again, it would wash up a thousand finds that no one had seen before, incongruous things that would end their journeys slumped on the beach, adorned with seaweed and rolled in sand; and tomorrow they would satisfy the curiosity of the truly bored.

Philip must have changed, I suppose. That, at least, was what the mother thought when she found that he was up and out of bed before her. At nine o'clock he was already outside, on the edge of the cliff, methodically searching the bay with his father's binoculars. She had to call him twice before he heard her. The coffee was ready.

Such a setting, such a beautiful view: he said he had found nothing like it anywhere, at least not in the United States . . . In fact, he would never go back there. Never. Finished. Done. When she heard this, the mother thought at first that it was a joke, the sort of news that has been so longed for that it has become implausible. It was the first time her son had ever really made her happy, especially that early in the morning.

He buttered a piece of bread, noticing – as he did – that his mother had not forgotten his preference for toasted baguette; but, before dipping it into his bowl of coffee, he asked in a rather less relaxed voice whether Boris had come back during the night.

'Well, I certainly didn't hear him. You know, I think that boy's a bit like you, he gets up late. At least, he doesn't strike me as an early bird.'

Even so, the mother did go on to say just how charming she thought his friend was, and how kind; he had done everything in his power to be pleasant and polite while waiting for Philip to arrive; a real pleasure to have around.

While she was on the subject she said how delighted she was that Philip had decided to get back in touch with old friends; it would do him so much good being with people like that – you know, healthy, sporty, dependable boys.

He drowned his bread with minute application, impressed yet again by the other man's perform-ance, the unanimous acceptance fabricated in little more than two days.

'Do you know, between you and me, I think that he and Julie . . . Well, I can't be sure of anything but . . .'

It gets better and better, he thought.

Particularly as the mother's face had brightened with explicit approval as she said these words.

'By the way, Mum, when he arrived, you did put him in the blue room, didn't you?'

'Yes, why?'

'How come his shutters are closed this morning?'

'Well, because he's asleep.'

'But they were still open at two o'clock in the morning, when we went to bed . . .'

'Well, he would have closed them when he got in, I suppose . . . he must have gone to bed later than you.'

Now things weren't going well at all.

The toast floated, dismembered, in the tepid coffee. He didn't want it any longer, but what he really must do was go and have a look upstairs.

'Well, aren't you going to finish it?'

In a shallow cavity in the cliff, above a cove where a number of pleasure boats had been anchored, André-Pierre and Philip were setting up the rockets for the evening. First, they had carried the cases right up to the top, then they used a winch to lower them very gently down the rock face, all in the full glare of the sun . . .

Philip was the foreman, and André-Pierre was reconciled to passing him the tubes one by one, even more cautious than usual, terrified by the thought of handling explosives. On top of that he had to endure constant criticism from an especially edgy Philip, who had not shaken off his anger since the morning.

'It can't get much worse, whatever made you go and do that?'

'I thought everyone would think: Ah, the shutters are closed, so he must be here . . .'

'And do you honestly think they would have gone on thinking that all day? Everyone would have looked up at his room all day thinking, Oh look, the shutters are closed, so he must be there, and everyone would have spent the whole day wondering just how long he would go on sleeping?'

'Well, I don't know, he could very easily have slept here last night, and left early this morning, I don't see why not . . .'

André-Pierre was backing down, like a

schoolboy losing his footing in front of a furious teacher. In fact, he now couldn't work out whether he had been right to close the wretched shutters, he had lost the thread of his own logic. In the end, he couldn't even remember how or why he could have thought it was a good idea. Just as he no longer knew whether it was genuinely hot, or if he was being overcome by fear, by the smell of gunpowder that filled him with lugubrious premonitions . . . Luckily Philip was in control, and this new Philip actually seemed quite sure of himself, which meant that prison really must have changed him a bit.

'And what if . . . ?'

'Just stop speculating . . . Anyway, it's too late now to back out.'

To Philip, what really mattered was that he'd got rid of the guy, got rid of the bastard who had become something of an obsession, who had infected his every thought. What mattered was to have found an outlet for his hatred in a crime that had so often been repressed; until then this hatred had been a blade tightly locked in the sheath of his conscience, but now that it had been used it could go on causing injury indefinitely.

'But are you sure he didn't have any relations, anyone who would be worried about him?'

'Pass those cables over there, come on, get a move on.'

The advantage, André-Pierre could see, was knowing that they were shot of him, that they had tossed him off like some minor nuisance. All through the night he had tried to cling to the idea that order had been restored – relieved that there was any form of order at all. But the sweating was starting again already, he felt trapped once more, penned in by the dozens of rockets attached directly to the rock; even the rock itself seemed to be seething, about to melt, ready to explode. Take the temperature up one more notch and the whole lot would blow.

'I really can't do this. You see, this sort of situation is just beyond me, I can't cope.'

'What about me? I suppose you think this kind of thing happens to me every day . . .'

'It's not the same for you, you'd had him on your back for months. And, anyway, people who've been in prison don't see things the same way.'

André-Pierre was convinced that a man who has spent time in prison is a breed apart, fundamentally altered; he can only emerge as a wild beast, raging, tainted by the furious, dark venom coursing through anyone who has been shut away. As far as he could see, Philip was not the same any more, prison had hardened him, as if it had vaccinated him against fear and indignation, immunized him against all emotion.

But Philip himself felt more fragile than ever,

177

haunted by the shipwrecked feeling he couldn't shake off, a feeling that had started in those first few hours, even in the first few seconds when they were questioning him and they told him to stay there, not to move, to ask if he needed to go for a leak . . . Deep down he had never understood how a few measly grams had sent him hurtling into such a vortex. Every morning when he woke up the same words came back to him: I don't believe it – until he shook or cried, like a little kid who doesn't want to play any more, begging for it to end . . . But no one in that place had paid any attention to his childish whims, the men there were all more hardened and cruel than each other, their hearts were as abrasive as the walls. The prisoners and the warders alike had all walked about without sweaters on when he felt cold; all winter he had been cold, eating, sleeping and peeing in the cold. While the others could only think about getting their hands on a mobile, a few cigarettes or some shit, he bartered for medicine that would bung him up, something to make him as constipated as possible, anything so that he didn't have to shit to the echoes of the other men . . .

In the early days, Boris had offered some respite: he seemed unshakeable, intelligent, and – most importantly – it was obvious he was not like the others. Boris had been the only coherent, dependable thing in the place, the only person he could really talk to, to the extent of even saying too much, even putting himself in the other's hands, describing a future filled with his boundless gratitude, asking for his protection as a sort of advance, in keeping with the proposed method of payment, an interest-free loan . . . Philip knew that it was a mistake to show such weakness, but he was prepared to make every kind of compromise and, right from the start, he had gauged the dangers of handing himself over to this guy, of asking for his guardianship; he had been well aware that sooner or later he would have to 'pay his dues', as Boris had put it, smiling as he had said it. Smiling – but not all that much.

'Yes, maybe, but at least you've been mulling this over for months, you've been thinking about this guy for months. But for me all this is new, I didn't even know him a couple of days ago . . . And this is all your problem, after all. At least, it's not mine . . .'

'Well, it is now.'

André-Pierre was haunted by the scene, everything about their surroundings here brought it back to him. Boris repeatedly disappearing under the water and then coming back up for breath, earnestly trying to find the wallet and credit card holder (another opportunity for him to show off), but each time he set off again towards the seabed the temptation came more sharply into focus: his outline became distorted before disappearing completely, it made you want him never to come back up, even to consider helping him on his way, even to wish, even to think . . . In fact, they did not even need to talk to know what each other was thinking; and although it was Philip who actually struck the blow, André-Pierre had been the one to point out the crowbar, already an accomplice.

The most sensible thing to do would be to start all over again, to rewind the film and watch it all again, to go back two days and avoid all this . . .

'What's done is done, for God's sake . . . And stop snivelling like that, or have a really good cry and then stop talking about it, but just give me a hand.'

André-Pierre went on handing him the rockets one by one. Philip concentrated on his pyro-technics with composure, with almost a sensual thrill, as if this form of danger suited him; he seemed to derive pleasure – a sense of grace – from being surrounded by all these little delayed-action bombs, as if he delighted in being so intimately acquainted with danger . . . be it fire, gunpowder, or even the memory of Boris . . .

André-Pierre was shaking more and more violently. Over and above the turmoil of emotion, and the anguish of a night spent listening for every tiny sound outside, and the need to keep combing over the bay since this morning to try to see every inch of it; over and above all that, he realized that he was nothing less than an accomplice to his hopelessly reckless brother-in-law . . . The very thought of this connection, the certainty that this sordid business had compromised him for the rest of his days, was enough to make him feel nauseous.

'Look, if this all goes wrong, I beg you, don't drag me into it. I'll give you anything you want but, whatever you do, say I had nothing to do with it. I mean it was you that hit him, I just showed you the—'

Philip leapt down from the rock and, almost falling, he took hold of André-Pierre's head, opened his mouth wide and rammed a firework between his jaws like a cigar, defiantly waving the flame of his lighter . . .

'And how much would you give me not to light this now, hey? Go on, name your price . . . Do you want me to tell you what you really are? Beneath all your airs and graces, you're just as bad as the other guy, just as disgusting, "the world owes you a favour", the only difference is that you think you can buy everything, and he just thought he could help himself.'

Towards the end of the afternoon they had a drink out on the terrace. Everyone was banking on Boris being back by suppertime; there were no two ways about it, he must have spent the night with some conquest, and now the weary conquistador would be brought back to them, not by the Gulf Stream, but by his own overriding desire not to miss the festivities.

Both Philip and André-Pierre heard the self-evidence of these assumptions with great relief. The idea of a sexual escapade – which no longer seemed to be in any doubt – was handled quite well by Vanessa; she thought it rather comical, almost amusing, whereas Julie seemed a little thoughtful, pretending not to care but having trouble disguising her disillusion.

A late afternoon in July has so much to recommend it: the sunlight still flooding everything but no longer aggressive, conversation flitting like a butterfly over the well-chilled drinks. It had been a good day so all that really mattered had been achieved, the rest could be treated as a recreation, in a different register, wearing different clothes; which was exactly why, before thinking about the meal, they would each go and have a shower and change for the evening.

They were all turned towards the house, Philip and André-Pierre had ended up opposite each other, each in a deckchair, not speaking, sealed by the same pact.

The sun beamed down on them as if from a searchlight, shining directly from the gateway into the park, sliding under the parasol and setting them ablaze with an enormous golden halo. It was going to be the perfect evening for setting off fireworks, not a single cloud, not a breath of wind, the realm of the sky was as peaceful as that of the sea below. They closed their eyes and savoured the total peace of this blessed time of day, a glass of champagne in their hands, the ice bucket on a low table, which reflected the dazzling sunlight. They poured themselves another glass, clinking them together in a languid toast, as if to some victory, a hard-earned peace, genuinely experiencing the well-deserved rest and recuperation of a warrior.

It must have been the shadow that intrigued them.

When a silhouette appears in the distance like that, between the gates to your property, when the shadow is projected all the way over to you, infinitely elongated, like a dark stain in the perfect light, you almost instantly feel suspicious.

At that time in the afternoon the sun blazed directly on to the terrace. Shielding their eyes with their hands, Philip and André-Pierre tried to discern the face, to identify the general silhouette, without really believing it . . . Still some way away, the man continued to walk towards them, not even pausing for a moment, he kept on coming at his steady pace . . . Philip was the first to sit up, not believing his eyes, while André-Pierre was already turning to stone, more paralysed now than he had been by the tetany.

The man walked towards them with the subtly exaggerated, slightly halting stride of someone who knows he is being watched. The images appeared as a series of reflections in his Ray-Bans: the emerald green lawn, smooth as velvet; the elegant house built of white stone, which over-looked the entire scene; the swimming pool at the bottom of a flight of steps; the transparent inflat-able chairs undulating on its surface; the teak sun loungers, empty once again.

It is hard to make out a man's intentions when you cannot see his expression, and it is in these circumstances that you project all your fears into this unseen expression, that you find in it every-thing you dread. As he drew closer, André-Pierre and Philip discovered their own reflection in his Ray-Bans, more twin-like than ever before; they saw themselves stand up, no longer knowing how to move or how to find the words. When he was level with them he tossed them a broad smile, the sort of carnivorous grin that is difficult to accept as genuine, a disarming expression. They both had the same idiotic reflex of putting their hands out to shake his . . . He did not respond, but drew up a chair next to them under the parasol, picked up a glass and held it out to them, as if waiting to be served, as if that was all he was there for . . .

'Right then, where were we . . . ?'

Only the father had seen everything from his room, just like in the days when he used to watch for the wild boar through the windows of his home, because there is a deep mistrust in man, particularly in a shooting man, a hunter; a mistrust that means he never stops hungering.

On the stroke of eight o'clock, the ironmonger went out to draw across the metal shutter. It was even hotter outside than inside. He glanced up at the sky: it was limpid, without a whisper of cloud, just the perfect trail of a very high aeroplane, straight and clear-cut with not the least breath of wind to make it deviate; not a sound except for the distant euphoric babble of the starlings, feeding on the wing high up in the evening sky. That was when he heard an explosion from the island, probably a rocket, the first one set off by the Chassagnes. A little odd, though, to be starting the fireworks when it was still light. He looked over towards the island, but could not see the tiniest glimmer of light in the sky, not the tiniest spark.

In fact, there was only one explosion that evening, a shot that did not produce the tiniest spark, the tiniest fizzle of colour, or the slightest expression of joy.

THE END

BEYOND THE GREAT INDOORS

Ingvar Ambjørnsen

'ARRESTINGLY ECCENTRIC'
Guardian

Frightened to answer the telephone? Nervous about what chaos awaits at the supermarket? Anxious Elling and his Neanderthal roommate are two social misfits learning, a bit late in life, how to live like normal average people after graduating from a halfway house. On a quest to make the most of their free-spirited new life, this odd couple embark on romancing the girl upstairs, becoming terrorist poets and taking an unforgettable road trip to the heart of the Norwegian countryside.

The perfect anecdote for cynics, *Beyond the Great Indoors* rejoices in the simple pleasures of friendship and reminds us of the importance of conquering our everyday fears.

The Oscar-nominated Norwegian film ELLING was based on Beyond the Great Indoors.

'UNHESITATINGLY RECOMMENDED'
Independent

'TOP TEN BEST NEW FICTION'
FHM

'ACCESSIBLE AND APPEALING'
Newsweek

0 552 77209 7

BLACK SWAN

SUBMISSION

Marthe Blau

You'll want to scream, but you'll be gagged.
You'll want to cry, but you'll be blindfolded.
You'll want to run away, but you'll be tied up.
You'll have no way of begging me, I'll do what I want
with you.

A story of sexual obsession, domination and extreme
desire, *Submission* tells of a young married Parisian
lawyer swept up in a cycle of sado-masochistic lust. A
handsome stranger she meets in the courts issues her
with a series of instructions which she finds herself
compelled to follow. As the violence of their
encounters escalates, these acts will become a
dangerous addiction that she can't break. But how
far can she go and how much of her life will she risk
in the process?

Based on the author's own story, *Submission* sent
shockwaves through the French establishment.

'THE BOOK'S CANDOUR RIVALS THAT OF
LA VIE SEXUELLE DE CATHERINE M'
Sunday Times

0 552 77237 2

CORGI BOOKS

THE SOCIETY OF OTHERS

William Nicholson

'HYPNOTIC, FAST-MOVING AND INTELLECTUALLY
CHALLENGING . . . QUITE STAGGERINGLY GOOD'
Daily Mail

He has nowhere to go . . . so he goes there.

An alienated young man can see no meaning in life. He
doesn't even see the point of getting out of bed in the
morning. To escape from his family he decides to set off
on a hitchhiking adventure around Europe, and is
picked up by a friendly lorry driver with an unusual
interest in philosophy.

The journey takes him through a violent and
Kafkaesque nightmare to a destination that changes his
life.

'A BAFFLING, STAGGERING, GRANDLY AMBITIOUS
WORK . . . QUITE REMARKABLE'
Time Out

'NICHOLSON WRITES WITH SUCH PANACHE THAT
THE SOCIETY OF OTHERS TRANSCENDS GENRES: IT
ENTERTAINS US WHILE IT REFLECTS WITH GREAT
PROFUNDITY ON THE HUMAN CONDITION . . .
ONE OF THE BEST NOVELISTS AROUND'
Piers Paul Read, *Spectator*

'NICHOLSON DESCRIBES IT AS "A THRILLER
ABOUT THE MEANING OF LIFE" AND THAT'S
PRETTY ACCURATE . . . A GENUINELY
THOUGHT-PROVOKING READ'
Mail on Sunday

0 552 77202 X

BLACK SWAN

3

A modern-day *Story of O*

Julie Hilden

Maya and Ilan have an unusual marriage: Maya agrees
to tolerate Ilan's chronic infidelity as long as she can
participate and he will never stray without her. To her
surprise, she finds their threesomes as arousing as they
are disturbing, and for a while, everything seems fine.
But as Maya's writing career takes off and she becomes
more independent, Ilan feels threatened, and opts for
another kind of sexual experimentation – one that plays
on Maya's fear and ultimately threatens her life.

A compelling chronicle of obessesion and power, *3*
brings new immediacy to a timeless question: What is
the greatest sacrifice you would make for love?

'IN THIS TERRIFIC DEBUT, JULIE HILDEN DOES
WHAT FEW WRITERS CAN OR DARE TO: SHE HAS
WRITTEN AN EROTIC, TRULY SEXY THRILLER.
3 IS SMART, SEXY, STRANGE, AND IMPOSSIBLE
TO PUT DOWN'
Dani Shapiro, author of *Family History*

0 552 77177 5

BLACK SWAN

A SELECTED LIST OF FINE WRITING
AVAILABLE FROM BLACK SWAN

77115 5	BRICK LANE	*Monica Ali*	£7.99
99313 1	OF LOVE AND SHADOWS	*Isabel Allende*	£7.99
77209 7	BEYOND THE GREAT INDOORS	*Ingvar Ambjørnsen*	£7.99
99946 6	THE ANATOMIST	*Federico Andahazi*	£6.99
77105 8	NOT THE END OF THE WORLD	*Kate Atkinson*	£6.99
99860 5	IDIOGLOSSIA	*Eleanor Bailey*	£6.99
77237 2	SUBMISSION	*Marthe Blau*	£6.99
77131 7	MAKING LOVE: A CONSPIRACY OF THE HEART	*Marius Brill*	£6.99
99767 6	SISTER OF MY HEART	*Chitra Banerjee Divakaruni*	£6.99
99935 0	PEACE LIKE A RIVER	*Leif Enger*	£6.99
99954 7	SWIFT AS DESIRE	*Laura Esquivel*	£6.99
77182 1	THE TIGER BY THE RIVER	*Ravi Shankar Etteth*	£6.99
77179 1	JIGS & REELS	*Joanne Harris*	£6.99
77177 3	3	*Julie Hilden*	£6.99
77082 5	THE WISDOM OF CROCODILES	*Paul Hoffman*	£7.99
77109 0	THE FOURTH HAND	*John Irving*	£6.99
77153 8	THINGS TO DO INDOORS	*Sheena Joughin*	£6.99
99996 2	EVA'S COUSIN	*Sibylle Knauss*	£6.99
77202 x	THE SOCIETY OF OTHERS	*William Nicholson*	£6.99
77106 6	LITTLE INDISCRETIONS	*Carmen Posadas*	£6.99
77093 0	THE DARK BRIDE	*Laura Restrepo*	£6.99
77145 7	GHOST HEART	*Cecilia Samartin*	£6.99
77204 6	SAINT VALENTINE	*Nick Tomlinson*	£6.99
99864 8	A DESERT IN BOHEMIA	*Jill Paton Walsh*	£6.99
99673 4	DINA'S BOOK	*Herbjørg Wassmo*	£7.99
77221 6	LONG GONE ANYBODY	*Susannah Waters*	£6.99
77101 5	PAINTING RUBY TUESDAY	*Jane Yardley*	£6.99
77201 1	K: THE ART OF LOVE	*Hong Ying*	£6.99